Deceit in the Sound

Miller's Pointe Romantic Mystery & Suspense, Book 2

Candice Jeneé

DEDICATION

All my fellow book lovers out there - our safe
spaces of books can never be taken away & I hope
some of you enjoy this one.

PROLOGUE

I'VE ALWAYS LOVED STORIES. They have always been my happy place. And, while I didn't have much in my life to escape from, I still loved having a place to escape to.

My family taught me a deep appreciation for books, and I spent many days of my young life in their book store, or in their home library. My grandmother always loved books, and my grandpa did everything to make sure she spent every day of her life surrounded by what she loved. Watching them share that love of story with the world in their little shop made me want to have my own bookshop one day.

And, even though their house has sold, and I opened up shop in their hometown rather than keeping their shop open a few towns over, I keep their memory alive in the spirit of my own shop.

My haven. My safe place.

THUD

At least, it was. I looked up startled at the sound coming from my back office. I grabbed the bat I kept behind the counter and moved toward the sound.

"Hello?" I called out.

Silence.

I tried the handle and pulled, opening the

door just in time to see a shadow running out the back door, into the shadows of the night.

I flipped on the light. The room seemed untouched, except the opened door and the desk, which was missing a drawer. There was also a fallen box of books.

Whoever it was, I interrupted them before they could do any damage. My heart was racing as I called the police.

Two deputy officers followed up, asked some questions, and said they'd let me know if anything happened. Then one of them, who looked oddly familiar, told me I should lock up and leave, in case the person came back.

I literally felt my heart break inside. My happy place was no longer a happy place, and I suddenly wondered if I'd ever feel safe again.

CHAPTER 1

I BREATHED INTO MY hands before fumbling to lock the door. Though it was almost the beginning of March, it was unseasonably cold for our little part of the Puget Sound. To me, that was strange after the unseasonably warm winter we'd had. Then again, I was a bookshop owner, not a weather girl. What did I know?

Despite the cold, the weather didn't call for rain that day, so I decided to ride my bike in to the shop. My car would have worked just as well, but I really needed as much activity as I could to work out my nervous energy after last night.

I rode down Oak Street toward the town square, and as I passed the Nautical Inn, I waved at one of their guests. I took in the brisk air and took a quick minute to tuck a stray strand of auburn curls under my beanie, my hands freezing since I'd forgotten my gloves. I could picture them, sitting on top of the entry table. Cold as it was, I was glad the warmth of summer would wait a bit longer. I preferred the spring and fall temps, but I'd take the cold if it meant we didn't have any scorching heat.

The tree lined town square was the hub of the town, built around the town hall. It's where most important shops can be found. Though it wasn't too early, there were still so few people out and about. The town typically got buzzing between eight and nine a.m., except for the students who were already in school by then or were already on their way to high school on the mainland. Even at the eight or nine o'clock hour, it still took a bit longer for people to be moving about. This town really came alive in the afternoon and evening hours.

The streets around town square were lined by evergreens and trees coming back to life with the colors of spring. Pink and red decorations still dotted some of the shops even though Valentines Day had been a couple weeks ago. The rest of the town was already transitioning to prepare for our March celebration of Whale Fest. Blues and teals and images of different kinds of whales and marine life were in place of those Valentine's decorations on some buildings.

Even though the main whale watching season wouldn't be until late spring through late fall, Miller's Pointe had a Whale Festival to kick off the season a few weeks early in the middle of March. March was prime time grey whale watching season, and we got many swimming past our island as Whale Fest was going on. It was always a big draw for tourists and locals alike. Also, any reason for the town to be festive and decorated brought us together. And, transitions between holidays always dragged on.

I inhaled the wonderful dark and rich aroma of coffee and signature sweet and spicy cinnamon rolls that filled the town square. The scents were coming all the way from Brew & Bake, the only bar and cafe in town - all in one. Thanks to Bud and Mabel, no one needed another place for food and gathering. I was always amazed at how far those smells could travel, across the parking lot and green space, right to our row of shops. The smell was incredible, but I was already running late. My stomach grumbled, reminding me I missed breakfast, making me want one of Mabel's famous cinnamon rolls all the more to ease the emptiness.

I skipped the cafe heading right to my shop. After locking up the bike, I managed to get the door unlocked even though my fingers felt as if they might fall off. I always loved the ride from the duplex to the shop, despite the bitter cold.

Opening the door, I flipped on the lights of The Bookshop and looked at my beautiful tree. Right in the front window of the shop was my year round Christmas tree, already decorated with purple, blue, and teal Whale Festival decorations. Though my favorite time of year had passed, my tree always helped me keep part of it alive all year through, for each holiday. Kids in town loved the twinkling lights and occasionally helping decorate the tree. It was a perfect way to light up the display window and special seasonal books.

For a minute, I watched as my dolphin and orca ornaments swam in the wash of blue twinkle lights. Then, I locked the door behind me and busied myself with the opening tasks. Late as I was, I only had ten minutes to complete them. However, I knew I'd likely have no visitors in the first hour, so I wasn't too worried.

I double checked the back door to ensure it was locked. After last night's issues, I was taking no chances. I straightened up the desk and fallen box of books, thankful the sheriff's office had let me open again today. I was still shaken up, but the store was my livelihood. The faster I could get to business as usual, the better.

Mornings at the shop were my favorite time of day. It was quiet. Everywhere. Most of the town seemed to be sleeping when I got up each day, but by the time I opened the shop at nine, there were usually people milling about. After completing my opening checklist - at least my quick version for late mornings - I unlocked the door.

Since I didn't expect a customer any time, I busied myself with some inventory paperwork in the back office. I kept the door cracked and kept an ear out for the front alarm chime. Having worked with my grandparents in their shop before they died and running this store on my own since they passed, I'd gotten used to most of the customer patterns, especially of this town. Right now, most customers would either be at the pub or the local shops that may open early.

Around 9:30 a.m., I heard the door chime sound. *Strange*, I thought.

"Be out in a second," I shouted as I finished the form in my hand.

When I came out of the office, I was face to face with the most handsome stranger I had ever seen.

"Hi, can I help you?" I greeted him when I found my voice again.

He looked in my general direction but didn't seem to focus on me until he got closer. His sandy blonde hair was in a close cut, longer on top but shorter on the sides, and it almost drew out the deep blue in his eyes. A scowl was in place on his lips in the midst of his scruffy facial hair.

As I approached, I noticed he was a good half a foot above my own height of five foot six. He was a very athletic looking guy and definitely wasn't from the island, if his tailored clothes and sun- kissed skin were any indication. His collared shirt was tucked into pressed, fitted jeans. When he moved, the shirt tugged over his musc5:30les, and I unfortunately found it very distracting.

"Is this The Bookshop? The store that was broken into last night?" He asked.

Word travels fast in this town, I told myself, looking around at all the shelves he seemed to be ignoring. *Even strangers hear things that happen.*

I knew I shouldn't be surprised. Growing up in such a small town, I knew how fast gossip could get around. I just didn't realize people had already heard about the break-in. Or, that a stranger would have heard so soon.

"Who are you? How did you know about that?" I blurted. I felt my cheeks redden immediately, surprising myself at my outburst.

"Sorry ma'am, Logan Hart," he said with the slightest drawl. Definitely not from around here. "I just opened up shop as a PI here in town. I heard that someone broke in from a local friend and a deputy friend. I thought I'd see if I could be of service to the store owner. Are they here?" His scowl deepened as he extended his hand to me.

"This is my shop. I'm Kassidy Winters." I shook his outstretched hand, noting he had a very strong grip. "I opened it a couple years ago. I'll keep all you said in mind, but nothing got taken and everything's in order, so I'm sure the police have it under control. Thanks for your offer, Mr. Hart."

"Would you mind if I browsed a bit? Snoop a little bit, as it were?" he asked, his expression finally softening.

Something about him nagged at me, but I couldn't put my finger on it. I didn't know what he expected to find, but I also wasn't quite ready to watch him walk out the door of my shop just yet.

"You can spend whatever time you want to here in the front, but we'll leave the back office to the police." I eyed him, slightly suspiciously, and slightly to get another look at his handsome features. My gut told me to trust him, but my heart told me to be wary of him.

He nodded his agreement, and just then the door burst open, the alarm chime filling the space between us.

My best friend, Bridgette rushed in. She was bundled from head to toe, her face barely visible between her beanie, scarf, and ear muffs. Even her chestnut hair was completely covered. But, her eyes were completely panicked.

"Griffin just told me what happened. Are you ok? Did they take anything? You were here when it happened? Why are you even open today? What's going on?" Her words were muffled by her scarf, and she stopped short when she noticed the handsome stranger. Untangling herself, she gave him a sideways glance before turning her attention back to me.

Word really did travel fast in our picturesque little water-locked town. Across a parking lot and green space from The Bookshop was Bake & Brew, the pub where Bridgette worked most of the time. That is, when she wasn't helping me or doing her own thing. She was extremely loyal and usually bubbly, and it came out, even now as she was worried about my shop and safety.

"I don't know what's going on, Bridge. Nothing was taken, but I interrupted him, or her, before they could do much. I'm ok, the store is ok, we're moving forward." I glanced at Logan.

Bridgette followed my eyes. We watched as he explored the store. I noticed he was using his hands a lot, especially at the plaques on the fronts and ends of the shelves. I knew the plaques had braille on them, but I'd never seen anyone use them. And, we didn't currently carry any braille books.

I made a mental note to change that in consideration of accessibility.

Logan moved toward us, as if to introduce himself to Bridgette, but more customers came in. As Bridgette and I were busy with some locals looking for specific books, Logan slipped out. It seemed as if he wanted to go unnoticed, but I'd been pretty good about keeping aware of my surroundings.

"Guess he didn't want to stick around," Bridgette said as the other customers left.

"Yeah, he was a little strange, kinda grumpy. He's new here. I've never seen him. He said he's a new PI and wanted to know about the break-in. Found out from a local friend or a deputy friend or something," I said.

My mind wandered to the blue eyed stranger, suddenly wishing he hadn't slipped out of the store. As much as I wanted to be wary of him, something about him felt completely safe. I wanted to feel safe right now.

"So, do you know anything about the break- in? Did they come after you? Were you in danger?"

"No, it's like, they didn't even realize I was here. Then, I scared him off. I have no idea what they were looking for. Nothing was taken, but I don't know if that was because I scared 'em or they didn't find what they were looking for."

"That's so scary," Bridgette said. "Especially after what happened before Christmas. I wonder what's going on around here. Do you think this time it's just you and The Bookshop, or do you think other places will be hit, too?"

It was a valid question. After everything had happened with our friends Calliope and Persephone just before Christmas, the town was on edge. We were all just starting to get back to normal. Most of us, anyway. Now, it was easy to question if I was a target, - like Calliope had been - or if someone was just targeting random businesses.

"I don't know, it's so weird. I felt so weird being here and having that happen. Like, I feel violated. This is supposed to be one of my safe places." I bit back tears as I said that.

Bridgette nodded, sympathy lighting her eyes. "Well, I gotta get over to the pub. I'm taking the brunch crowd before having to go back for the night crowd. I'll check in with you later. Maybe stop by for lunch and some hot chocolate. I'll save you a cinnamon roll. It's definitely the perfect day for hot chocolate and a cinnamon roll."

She pulled the scarf back up around her mouth and nose, as if emphasizing the perfect day for hot chocolate part. I nodded and we waved to each other as more customers came in.

I definitely considered the offer, especially with the promise of a warm, fragrant cinnamon roll. My stomach grumbled in response.

The rest of the day went as usual. I did go to lunch at the pub before coming back to the afternoon lull at the store. By the time I locked up at the end of the day, I was exhausted and had almost forgotten about the break-in the night before.

Chapter 2

I vaguely heard the phone ring, and my eyes fluttered open.

"Hello?" I whispered, as I looked at the clock. *5:30 in the morning? What's happening?*

"Ma'am, this is Deputy Kinkaid. Do you own The Bookshop on Miller's Pointe?"

Panic gripped me and I sat straight up. I was wide awake now. Not again, I thought.

"Yes, I do. What happened?"

"I'm afraid there's been another break in. I need you to come down here right away. We need your help assessing the scene and letting us know if something is missing." He was calm but firm, causing a rush of adrenaline to spike again.

"I'll be there in twenty minutes." I didn't even know if I'd hung up the phone or not.

I sprung out of bed and threw on my leggings and a tunic. I wouldn't normally wear sneakers to work, but I knew there would be a mess. I grabbed a hat and hurried out the door, almost forgetting to lock it behind me.

When I arrived at the store, I was trying to calm myself. There's hardly ever been any real crime in our small town. Except a few months before when the Fosters were killed and their granddaughter, Calliope was tormented and attacked. Before that, even with all the weird and questionable people around, crime was usually small and infrequent.

Why me? Why The Bookshop? Twice in just as many days. And, with nothing anyone could even really want? My mind was going a million miles a minute.

The first thing I noticed was the artisan picture glass door shattered and the door frame broken. Glass was everywhere. It took a moment to register the scene. Beyond the broken door, I saw the deputies looking around the store. I carefully stepped over the threshold of my now destroyed door that was held open by a stack of books.

"Excuse me, I'm Kassidy Winters. I own this shop," I greeted one of the deputies.

"Yes, Miss. Winters, let me take you to talk to Deputy Kinkaid."

He walked me over to another deputy who seemed to be in charge. His look definitely matched the voice on the phone. Gentle but commanding. Law enforcement suited him.

"Miss. Winters. So sorry to have to call you down so early in the morning. Someone heard the commotion and called it in. When we arrived, the person was gone; and if you have it, your security system seems to be down."

"They shut down my security system? But I have an alarm and a camera. How could they have turned them off?"

He shook his head, concern all over his face. I took a second to study his features, recognizing him as one of the deputies who had been around a few times when everything was happening with Calliope in December. He was handsome enough, but not quite my type. *Bridgette, however,* I thought to myself.

I shook my thoughts free, forcing myself to focus on what he was saying. Someone had disarmed the security and then broken in. Again. A shudder went up my spine as he continued.

"I'm not sure why, and we haven't found any equipment for that sort of thing. We're also not sure if anything is missing, so we need you to check it all out. Whoever did this got into the safe and overturned everything from the desk, so maybe start there."

Deputy Kinkaid led me into the back office, where I saw another disaster. My heart sank and I had to fight off tears. Again. Whatever the intruder had been looking for the other night, he or she came back to try again. I still had no idea what they were after, and that bothered me. If I'd known of something truly valuable, that would have made it all so much easier.

As it was, all I had to my name was tied up in this shop, and now it was all crashing down around me. Looking at the mess, who knew how long I'd have to close. I couldn't afford that. Not when I was so close to my final payment to put the place in my name. I knew my landlords would be merciful, they were some of my closest friends after all, but still.

I checked the safe first. At first glance, it looked like the money and documents were still there. Everything just looked like it had been shuffled around.

"Am I safe to start putting things back? Looking through things?" I asked Deputy Kinkaid, not wanting to disturb any evidence.

"Yes ma'am, they've processed what they can back here and moved on to the front room. I'll be around, just let me know if you find anything missing."

He ducked back out to the front, and I turned a slow circle around me. Overwhelmed by the mess, I found myself wishing I wasn't doing this alone. I took a minute to count the money from the safe, and then looked through all the documents. Nothing was missing. I replaced the items as they had originally been and closed the safe.

Moving on to the desk, I focused on putting things back in their proper drawer. I didn't bother to organize them as they had been. There was time for that later. I just wanted to find out if anything was missing. I began with the bottom drawer on the left side and worked my way up and around the desk. Nothing was missing.

"So, ma'am, anything missing back here?" Deputy Kinkaid stood in the doorway, watching me process the scene around me.

"I don't think so, not that I can tell. This place was a bit disorganized recently, so it may take a bit more time, but I really don't think so." I put the last drawer in the desk, and looked over at the shelves where I kept extra inventory. Everything on that side of the room appeared untouched.

"Nothing back here is missing. Money, documents, inventory. Everything's here. It's just a mess. Can I check around the register and counter area? The shelves out there will need a lot more time than I'm sure you have right now."

The deputy went to check the front, and I took a deep breath. My mind started going into overdrive at the thought of all I would need to do to prepare for business again. Tears were even closer this time.

"Ma'am," he waved me over, and nodded toward the counter.

"You know, you're probably older than me, and I'm young. You really don't need to call me ma'am. Kassidy will do just fine," I teased Deputy Kinkaid. I had a feeling it was just in his nature, considering he had a thick southern drawl. This crime seemed to be bringing them out of the woodwork.

He confirmed my suspicions when he said, "can't do that, ma'am. My momma would never let that slide. Older or not."

He winked and a smile lit up his face. Oh boy, if Bridgette ever had a run in with this man, he'd give her a run for her money.

I laughed at the thought as I made my way to the counter area. I checked the register first. It had been left open, much like the safe and the desk. I quickly counted the money and found it was all there. I searched all the cubbies in the cabinet, and a knot settled in the pit of my stomach.

My spare keys.

"Well, all the money and everything is still here," I told Deputy Kinkaid, "But they seem to have taken my spare keys. It had a key to the shop, a key to my house, and another key that I'm not sure what it was."

Concern washed over his face as he jotted a note in his notebook. The knot in my stomach tightened, and now I really wish someone was here with me. More specifically, I found myself wishing Logan was here with me, helping me handle the ugliness. Looking for his own clues to catch this person. Not that I didn't trust the deputies.

"It will take me a while to do inventory and see if anything else is missing, but I doubt it. I don't have any valuable books here or anything like that. It looks more like someone just broke in to make a huge mess and steal my keys. Whatever they were looking for was clearly not here. Do you think they'll be trying my house?"

"I'm not sure. I think we have all we need right now, though. We'll get our report written up, and we'll contact you with any questions we have or leads we find. You do the same for us, all right? Oh, and also, we'll have some officers do extra duty driving by your house today, but I suggest getting those locks changed."

I gave him a knowing nod, not wanting to think about what could come next. I continued trying to fight off the tears, almost unsuccessfully. "Of course, thank you. I will do all of that. Am I able to get the store back in order now that you're done? I can't really afford to stay closed long."

He nodded, and my tears threatened even more.

God, this store is my life. I bought it with everything that was left of my grandparents' legacy. Their wish for a bookstore on the island, and it's all around me in ruin. God, what am I going to do? I silently prayed.

This was almost more than I could take, and just at that moment, Bridgette rushed in.

"Oh my gosh! Not again. What happened here?" She wasn't talking to me. I knew because she wrapped me in her arms, but I knew her eyes were leveling Deputy Kinkaid.

"A break-in, ma'am," his calm voice responded. "And you are?" There was a mock accusatory tone to the question. Clearly, he was teasing her. Wrong move with my best friend, but I listened for what I knew would come next.

She let go of me to face him fully. "I'm her best friend. And this is the second time this has happened here. What are you doing to make sure it doesn't happen again, Deputy?"

"Oh, Kinkaid, ma'am. Trust me, I'm doing what I can. We've gotten all we can get now. Got all the pictures and prints we think we can. We'll just go ahead and get out of your hair so you can do what you need to do." He looked around Bridgette to me, "Kassidy, a pleasure. Bridgette, stay out of trouble, ma'am."

A smile played on his lips as he tipped his cap and left. Bridgette turned all sorts of shades of red, out of both anger and attraction, I'd guess. I laughed, and it was nice for a moment apart from the chaos.

"Okay, what do we know?" Bridgette turned back to me, back to business.

"I don't know." I shook my head, tears finally finding their way down my cheeks. "Bridge, they didn't take anything except keys?" It came out more as a question.

It was so strange. Until the community center fires and Calliope's stalker, crime was basically non-existent in our sleepy little town. Of course, the Gideons were always sketchy, but mostly didn't harm anyone. Other than that, it would be petty crimes or harmless teenage pranks, and even that was infrequent.

But this? Someone had taken time with the alarms and cameras only to take my spare keys. It didn't make any sense.

"They took keys?" Bridgette asked, worry all over her face.

"I keep a set of spares here. One for the house and one for the shop. And one more that I don't quite remember where it goes. Maybe an old storage place my grandparents owned. It's the only thing that's gone."

I felt like something else must have been taken. That was a lot of work for a set of keys. Still, I honestly couldn't figure out what else it could be.

I picked up a shattered picture frame that held the smiling faces of my grandparents, who had opened their own bookstore over in Marysville over fifty years ago. Later, they helped settle Miller's Pointe, but commuted to their shop in Marysville. Their dream was to open a small shop here too, which I carried on. And now, it was falling apart before my eyes.

Bridgette and I silently settled into starting to put the shop together. She began replacing books on shelves, while I pulled up the inventory program on the iPad and followed behind.

While we worked, Joe, one half of the town's contractor couple, came to look at the door. He promised to have it fixed the next day. In the meantime, he was going to board it up and fix up the frame to keep out unwanted guests and the elements. No telling what Washington early spring weather would do this time of year, which wasn't great for a store full of books.

A few hours later, we had finished a small corner of the store, seeing some progress in getting it back in order. As expected, everything was accounted for. I suspected the rest of the store would be the same.

"Let's go to Brew & Bake for a break, and let these guys finish their work with the door," Bridgette suggested, tugging on my sleeve. She looked as exhausted as I felt. I nodded my agreement. Grabbing my purse, which I'd miraculously remembered on the way out of my house this morning, I followed Bridgette across to the pub.

CHAPTER 3

WE ARRIVED AT BREW & Bake and found Griffin working on his laptop in our usual booth. The round booth was in a back corner of the main room, just outside view of the windows that lined the front of the pub. Most of the walls of the main room were covered in pictures, signs and knick-knacks. This one was no exception. There was even a picture of many of the town's founding members, including Calliope's grandparents. The whole place was eclectic and homey, a perfect eatery for a small, close-knit town.

"It happened again," I said, with tears in my eyes again. I slid into the booth on the other side of Griffin without even asking. Bridgette scooted in next to me.

"What happened again?" he asked, closing his laptop. As the newspaper man of the town, he showed great confusion at being behind in the big news of the day. Especially news that upset his friend so much. That last part may have had more to do with his soft heart than the news, though.

"A break in," Bridgette filled in, adjusting in the spot next to me.

"I just don't understand, nothing was missing. He didn't take anything except my spare keys, but he was definitely looking for something. And, that something is bigger than just keys. I know it. I just have no idea what it is."

"Kassidy, I'm so sorry." Concern covered Griffin's face, as he patted my hand sympathetically.

"He did leave a huge mess. But, we're working to get it back in order. And, they are coming to replace the door soon." I laid my head on the table.

Bridgette picked up the story. "Joe's got it covered. He said he'd replace it for free, and the team's coming tomorrow with the glass. They are over there now, putting boards up. He suggested she get a metal gate for the front of the store to help with security, since the jerk somehow disabled her alarms and cameras."

I could feel her bouncing as she told the story. I marveled at her unending energy. I just felt drained from everything; ready to crawl into a ball in bed.

"That's all really strange. Why would someone go through all the trouble to shut down alarms, break in, and then take nothing but keys?" Griffin asked, his journalist brain beginning to work. He took a drink of his tea and then tapped his pen against his laptop.

Griffin's family owned the Miller's Pointe newspaper, as well as a few others in the Pacific Northwest. Anything like this always piqued his interest. He saw it as a journalistic challenge or puzzle.

I just shook my head, barely bothering to lift it off the table. None of it made any sense. I was not enjoying the process of putting the store back in order and hated that I'd lost a whole day because of it. And, that I would still lose business until I could re-open.

Sensing it was all too much, Bridgette blurted, "so, Griff, who's this new guy?"

I looked up, much more interested in this than my break in. More interested than I would care to admit, and I hoped Griffin didn't notice how I'd reacted to her question.

Griffin stared at Bridgette, then looked to me, and back at the Bridgette. "The new guy? But, what about the break-in?"

"Look, that's all a lot right now. Time to change the subject, so, spill. He was in the book shop yesterday asking all kinds of questions, and poking around about the first break-in. You seem to know him, so…"

Bridgette let her sentence fall, waiting for Griffin to fill in the blanks. Always one to speak her mind, Bridgette had no problem voicing the questions she and I both undoubtedly shared. I was always thankful for my bubbly and outgoing friend.

"What makes you think I know him?"

"Griffin, I work here. Nothing in this town goes past me," she rolled her eyes. I nodded to remind him that Bridgette was the town's best source of information. Even better than him and his paper.

"He's a new PI in town…" Griffin started.

"You mean, the only PI?" Bridgette cut in. "Since when is there enough crime in this town to call for a PI? I mean, besides the obvious. Have you figured out why he came here? It's so weird and makes no sense."

"Well, I think the lack of anything bigger than petty crime until a few months ago is something that drew him here, but you'd have to let him tell you the whole story.

He was a cop for a while, then got into investigative journalism. He was a pretty good one too, until his injury. He made a new career choice that brought him here." Griffin shrugged.

I thought about our new neighbor. No wonder he was so interested in the break-in. Coming to a small town, likely expecting very little criminal activity, only for a pretty major event a couple weeks in. Not the quiet life I imagined he was going for.

"I wonder if he's any good," I said absently as I stared out the closest window.

"Let's hope so. Let's get Calliope and team up with him and get to the bottom of this." Bridgette said, excitement in her voice. Griffin nodded in agreement. I just shook my head.

"You want to bring Calliope in to help? You? You really want to do that?" I was surprised she even thought that.

"She's the one who figured out everything to keep everyone alive last time, didn't she? I wouldn't say we're best friends now or anything, but, she's crazy. She's brave, and she runs headlong into danger to protect people. Sounds like someone we could use here, doesn't it?"

I knew my friends well enough to know they wouldn't let it go. Callie wouldn't let it go once she knew more about it, either. Bridgette loved a good adventure, while

Griffin and Calliope couldn't let go of a good puzzle. But, I had no desire to be a PI. Especially after what happened to Callie in December. I preferred fictional adventure to all this real life tragedy.

"Or, you know, we could just let the Deputy Kinkaid and the police detectives do their jobs, right?" I said, hopeful.

Bridgette and Griffin shook their heads in unison, and Bridgette mumbled something. I sighed in response. My friends always persuaded me to go along with their antics, but this time, I felt uneasy about it. I didn't have much time to come up with an argument against it, because Calliope came in just at that moment.

"Blondie, over here," Bridgette waved her over.

A look of annoyance shown on Callie's face as she approached. We all knew she hated the nickname, but it wasn't going away any time soon. There was still too much tension between her and Bridgette.

"I've asked you not to call me that, please. Let's just move past it." Callie took off her coat and slid in next to Griffin, as far away from Bridgette as she could get.

"Sorry. Okay, look, we need your help with something. You heard about the break in yet?" Bridgette leaned forward excitedly. I started to think she was feeling left out of the last mystery adventure.

"Perse just told me this afternoon. I went by the shop, but you were here. So, how are you? I'm so sorry. I'm sure it must feel like some sort of violation." True understanding shown on her face. After the last couple months, I knew she was one of the few who could relate to the fear rising inside me.

"It does, and it sucks," I said, ready to move away from the topic.

"So, what can I do?" Callie asked, reaching for the order pad and writing an order.

"Well," Bridgette started, "Griff here has a new friend in town, a PI. We want to team up with him and solve this thing. Keep our girl here safe. Want in? Another puzzle to solve."

For a second, what looked like anger flashed in Calliope's eyes, but it melted into something else, something softer. I couldn't quite read where her thoughts were going,

"Sorry, too soon?" Bridgette sank back, realizing maybe there hadn't been enough time that had passed since the last time Calliope had to keep someone safe.

"It's just been a rough couple months, and finishing out the school year on the mainland, commuting every day; it's just a lot. But, yeah, I'll help however I can. I feel like

I'm cursed. Like I brought evil to town, and now it won't leave."

A tear rolled down her cheek, and she quickly wiped it away. Griffin put a protective arm around her, and we grew quiet. It really had been a rough couple of months since the town had lost her grandparents.

"Okay, Kass, we're all in. Let's get to know this new Logan guy, and get solving. No one threatens one of us without threatening all of us," Bridgette said. Griffin and Callie nodded in agreement.

"Fine, let's figure it out, I guess," I said as I took the order pad from Callie and wrote down my order, passing it to Bridgette. I had a feeling I might regret it, but life with my friends was always an adventure.

Griffin had an interview in Seattle with someone for one of his family's papers, so he left us to our own chatting. He was kind enough to take our order to the bar for us. As soon as he was out of earshot, Bridgette turned and asked, "so, do either of you know anything about him?"

"I don't know much," I said, playing with the order pad and salt shaker in front of me.

"Calliope?" Bridgette asked.

Calliope shook her head. "I didn't even know we had someone new in town. Man, going to the mainland every-day really keeps me out of the loop."

"Come on, Kass, I know you've done some research beyond what he's told you. I know you."

"Ok, I may have done a little research after he came into the shop. His name is Logan Hart. He went to school for journalism, but then became a cop. He left that to go back to investigative journalism. He was partially blinded on assignment when someone hit him in the back of the head. They thought his full sight would come back, but it hasn't happened yet. He got his PI license and moved here to work. Also, never married, still looking for the suspect who blinded him, and he's obviously been a little cranky since he got hurt. That last one I'm just guessing based off my interaction with him."

"Wow, that must be so hard. Obviously he was good at what he did, and then to have it all fall apart like that." Calliope shook her head and gave me a knowing look, likely thinking of her own health issues and mood.

"I'd probably be cranky, too," Bridgette snorted. "Los-ing part of your sight doing something you're great at, and then it all falls apart. Yeah, that'd piss me off, I'm sure."

"Yeah, his moodiness makes sense, but how would you know. You've never been cranky a day in your life." Sarcasm dripped from my words. It felt good to joke with my friends. Joking took the edge off the anxiety of everything else.

"I was cranky once. A long time ago. I didn't like it, so I stopped." Bridgette smiled widely and winked at us, laughing at Calliope's grimace.

"So, why did he choose here? You guys trust him?" Callie asked.

"Something about him screams trustworthy, but I don't know," I said. "I mean, the store was broken into so soon after he came to town. How weird is that? I honestly don't know if it's coincidence."

"What's a coincidence, sweetie?" Mabel's soft voice broke our conversation, and she put a hand on my shoulder before passing out our drinks. I had almost forgotten other people were around.

"Just some things about the break-in at The Bookshop," Bridgette filled in Mabel.

Mabel and Bud were Bridgette's godparents, and the owners of Brew & Bake. Mabel and her husband had built Brew & Bake from the ground up. They were one of the cutest couples in town, still happily working together after so many years.

Mabel patted me on the shoulder again, lowering the tray to her side. "I was one of the ones who had to call the police. I'm so sorry I didn't let them know in time. I'm so, so sorry. Is there anything I can do to help?" Mabel would have moved the earth and sun for anyone in town, but I knew we girls had a special place in her heart.

I shook my head. "Thank you, Mabel. And, thank you for calling the police. You're a guardian angel if ever there was one. You be safe here early in the mornings, ok? Maybe have someone come in early with you and Bud to help you both out until this is all sorted?" Concern marked all our faces around the table.

Brew & Bake wasn't too close to The Bookshop, but everyone knew Mabel, and usually Bud, came in really early to get going on things for brunch and all the desserts. She made them fresh daily, often with the help of Bridgette, too. Anyone in town would be happy to come help them in the morning. If someone was out prowling so early, other than the hotel, Brew & Bake would be the only business open. I didn't feel very safe for any of us at the moment.

"Oh, pooh," Mabel said with the wave of her hand. "No one wants to come here and help an old couple work the pub in the morning. Everyone's got too much going on in their own lives. No girls, we're fine. We've lived a lot of years. Not much scares me or Bud anymore."

We nodded at Mabel. I suddenly realized how dangerous it could be for other business owners if someone did to them what had been done to me the other night. I worried for the town. Break ins like this just never happened so close to home.

"Ok, Bridgey-girl, you have a shift in ten minutes. Don't make me dock you late pay." Mabel snapped the rag she'd had in her apron at Bridgette before walking away with a laugh. Everyone knew full well Mabel wouldn't be docking Bridgette's pay. Even on the days she was late.

Bud came over with our food, but at that moment I realized just how little appetite I'd had. I nibbled at my food while the others ate, Bridgette practically inhaling everything at once.

"Well, I'm going to go check on the progress at the store, and then head home, I guess. No sense in trying to run my business today. I need a bath and a good book now. Luckily, I have both at home."

"Want me to go with you?" Calliope offered.

"No, really, it's okay. I'll be fine." I swallowed down the rest of my drink as quickly as I could, pulling out my wallet to leave my pay. Both my friends waved me away, and I didn't argue.

"Ok, I'll call you tonight," Bridgette said, "and I'll send Ben over with some dinner. He's running deliveries tonight. Don't leave your place again today. Let us come over and take care of you. You take it easy."

She squeezed my hand before heading toward the back room to start work.

"Look Mabel, five minutes early," she said dramatically, loud enough for the whole dining room to hear.

Callie shook her head, turning back to me, "so, how are you really doing?"

"I don't know. I think we all thought what happened at the community center was a one off thing, but now?" I shook my head. I didn't want to burden her after everything she'd been through. I started putting on my coat, ready to leave, but willing to chat for a bit longer.

"Well, don't let anyone try to tell you you did it to yourself, because, that's just infuriating." Callie let out a sad laugh.

"So far, that hasn't happened yet, but I can imagine that sucked. I'm sorry. How are you doing?"

"There are good days and bad, but hey, we press on. We got all the permits and everything to move forward on the community center. I have your dad and a plumbing contractor coming out in a few days to start their part of everything. Does he know yet what happened?" Callie asked.

She took a drink of her soda, as Bridgette came over and cleared our plates. Bridgette gave me a quick side hug before going back behind the bar.

"I haven't told my parents anything. I don't really want to tell them, but he installed the security system, so I probably need to let him know." I sighed. This wasn't a conversation I was ready to have with my parents.

"Well, go home and get some rest. Maybe you'll be ready to call them after you've had a quiet night at home and a good night's sleep."

"You might be right." I picked up my scarf and wrapped it around my neck.

I waved goodbye to Callie, just as Trent joined her at the booth. He gave her a sweet kiss and settled in with his hand on hers over the table. It was like they were the only two in the world.

I warmed inside. It was nice to see that even in the times of tragedy, new relationships could form and grow. Everyone in town loved how cute those two were together.

If I wasn't so anxious about the break-ins, I might have been a little envious of my friend. I know Bridgette was. But, there was no denying, these two were great for each other. Someday, it would be my turn, too.

Chapter 4

Getting back to The Bookshop, I found Joe loading up his truck. None of his other workers were around.

"Well?" I asked.

"We got it all boarded up. We'll be back in the morning with a better lock system for you, but we got a temporary one set up. I really want you to think about getting that metal grate. If anything happened to you, or this place, I just don't know what I'd do. You know, we're all here lookin' after you."

I nodded. Joe had been one of my dad's best friends growing up. They seemed to have drifted apart when my parents moved away to do other things but were still friendly. When I opened the shop on the island, Joe always took it upon himself to take care of me when I needed anything.

"I know. Hey, can we also change all the locks on the duplex, too? The only thing they took were my spare keys. I have no reason to believe they know where I live, but, better safe than sorry, right?" I shrugged.

"Absolutely. I'll take care of that tomorrow, too. The town's got their eye out, now, you know. This guy won't get away with it in your shop or any other shop anymore."

"Thanks, Joe. See you tomorrow."

After waving goodbye, I inspected the work done on the front of The Bookshop. Seeing it boarded up broke my heart. Thinking of the money it cost to be closed gave me a headache.

Rather than going home, I went to the town historical society which also served as a local library. I knew it would be open since they were open Mondays, Wednesdays, and Fridays. If I couldn't be around the books in my own shop, I'd go to the other place where books lived in this little town. I knew I could just do some work with the reference desk and give Stella a much needed break.

"Kassidy!" Stella greeted louder than she should have, though we were likely the only two in the place at the moment. "Are you all right? I've heard about everything that's been happening. I'm so sorry." Stella pulled me into a hug.

Though I was expecting it, I was never quite prepared for the bear hugs Stella used to greet others.

"It's been rough. I thought I'd come in and do some busy work. Take my mind off things. Any returns need to be shelved or any new exhibits to set up or cycle out? Need a break?"

"I don't need a break, Kyle packed me a lunch today." Stella blushed at the mention of her new husband. "And, we haven't been busy since it's the off season. But, I'll gladly let you help me with re-shelving books so I can take care of some of our fundraiser and financial work that I'm behind on."

"You got it."

Whale season being around the corner meant the town's two biggest fundraiser events were on the horizon. She usually found a lot of work to do for those this time of year. She always tried to get as much prepared during the off season as she could.

I found the returns cart loaded with books. Obviously it had been several weeks since anyone restocked the shelves. I had never been more thankful for someone's lack of organization in my whole life.

Rounding the corner to the resources section, I spotted Logan at one of the resource tables, a book open, and an ear piece in one ear. Approaching cautiously, I tried to decide the best way to get his attention. I decided a simple greeting was best.

"Uh, hi. Logan, right?"

Logan startled a bit and looked up at me. I was taken aback again by his charming look. Something about the way he focused on me made me a little fluttery.

A smile lit up his scruffy face. "Hey, owner of the book store. Kassidy, right?" He asked, but I felt like he already knew.

"Yes, that's me."

"Sorry about the second break-in. Griffin told me. How are you holding up?" He asked. Though there was an edge to his voice, I picked up genuine concern in what he'd asked.

"Thanks, uh, I'm shaken up. Really, just feel, I don't know, violated. Is that weird?" The words were out of my mouth before I could stop them. I was usually more guarded, close to the vest with strangers. Logan put me at ease, even if I didn't want to admit it.

"No, not weird at all. Why don't you take a seat?" Logan gestured in front of him.

I wanted to keep my guard up, to not trust this Logan, but there was something about him that I couldn't help but trust. Something familiar, almost. I took the seat across from him, leaving the book cart all but forgotten.

"What are you doing?" I asked, cheeks warming at the flutters I was feeling talking to him.

"I'm doing some research for a case. Though not quite the fast-paced adventure of what's happening around here, it's keeping me busy all the same." I sensed teasing in Logan's voice, and it sent my heart racing.

I internally chastised myself for my response to him. I was supposed to be the level- headed one, and Bridgette was supposed to be the love-struck, gooney eyed one. For Bridgette up until recently it was a new guy every season. But me? I was the bookish one who was never swayed by a guy. Not even good-looking detectives who seemed to want to help me.

"It's definitely an adventure around here, all right. One I wish I wasn't at the center of this time. Bridgette lives for drama and adventure. I'd rather have my adventure in fiction form, thanks."

Logan laughed. "You sound like my mom. When I joined the force, she told me, "Logan, now, I'll always love you, but you can get more adventure in a good book than you can get on the force. And much safer, to boot." Apparently, safer than investigative journalism, too," he said absently, but his smile dismantled any tiny lack of trust I was holding onto.

"Are you a reader, then?" I asked him.

"Not as much anymore. I listen to a good audiobook every now and then. But, not a reader like you clearly are. Closed up the bookshop for the day and came to the closest thing to a library the town has. That's a book lover if I ever met one."

"I help out here sometimes. Stella works here alone, except when the town brings in someone to do the books. I do come in to help as often as I can, even bringing in books from time to time, especially for the kids. I love it. But, I didn't close up by choice. Someone made that choice for me," I reminded him.

"Well, when will you be able to open the shop back up?" Logan asked. I was still hesitant to let him work on the case, but part of me was starting to like how interested he was.

"Uh, a few days, I think. Joe, the one fixing the door, is going to do all the work there, and then come replace the locks at my house."

"Why your house lock? Did your home get broken into, too?" Logan straightened up, as if needing to be alert. Like he needed to be ready to act.

"Well, whoever it was, only took my spare keys that were kept at the store. Nothing else. Not sure why. But, Joe is going to change the locks for me, just in case." I paused a moment, a thought struck, and I let it out without a second thought, "Wait, did you already know the keys were missing?" I asked, wondering if I'd trusted Logan too soon, my mind running ahead of me.

"What?" He looked confused more than offended. Of course, he didn't know the keys were missing. Or maybe he did, because Griffin told him. Not because he'd done anything. My cheeks reddened from embarrassment.

"I don't know. I'm sorry. I'm so on edge, I shouldn't accuse you of breaking into my store. You've just been trying to help, albeit abrasively at times. And, here I am questioning you. I'm sorry."

"Is that what you were doing? Accusing me?" he asked with a light laugh. "Thanks for apologizing. And, well, abrupt is kind of how I am at times. My social skills aren't always the best. At least you admitted you think it could have been me. But, I'm glad to let you know it wasn't. I really just came here to do a job and start a new life."

"I'm sorry again. This is just so unusual for our town..."

"Is it, though? What about the fires a few months ago? That's a pretty big deal, right?" He cut in.

"You're right. But, before that, all unusual for our town. And to have this kind of thing happen twice, to me, I just feel like I'm the target." I felt the tears welling up again. Willing myself not to cry in front of Logan, I said, "I'm going to get back to my task now. It was nice to talk to you."

"Before you go, take my card. If anything happens. If you need me at all, please call me. My phone is always on, and I rarely sleep. Also, I'm a perfect shot, even half blind." He winked at me, not yet knowing how much winking disturbed me.

I took his card and put it in my back pocket as I began re-shelving the books. Once I had finished the entire cart, I said a quick goodbye to Logan, and one to Stella on the way out.

I was ready for a good book and my bath tub. Ben would be bringing my dinner soon, too. Yes, a relaxing evening ahead was exactly what I needed.

Chapter 5

I RETURNED HOME FROM the longest day I'd had in a while. Stopping short, my heart sank. My door was cracked open.

I took a deep breath. *Not again. Not my home*, I thought to myself as I pushed the door wide. Now I knew I'd been wrong about them knowing where I lived. I also realized I was definitely the target. I just had no idea why.

A huge mess greeted me. The extremely organized person I was couldn't handle it. I reached for the umbrella I kept by the door, relieved to find it still in its place. Holding it up like a bat, I slowly made my way through the house. I was too angry with this intruder to be scared to encounter him. No one was there.

Before I even called the police, there was only one person I thought to call.

"Hello?" His voice answered, putting me at ease immediately.

"Logan?" I asked.

"Yes. Kassidy?" Just hearing him say my name made my heart turn and gave me hope for safety in that moment.

"Someone broke into my house. Or, I guess, they didn't break into it, they used the key. It's been tossed and searched."

"Did you go in alone?" He asked. I could hear shuffling, like he was gathering himself. He was coming to me.

"I, uh, yeah. I did. No one is here, but I'm still scared."

"Text me your address then call the police. I'll be right there."

"Got it, thanks so much."

As soon as I called police, I called Bridgette at the pub.

Within minutes, Bridgette was at my door, before the sheriff even arrived. Shortly after Bridgette, Griffin arrived with Logan. The deputies finally arrived minutes later. They must have already been close to the island.

"Miss Winters, how unfortunate to see you again. I see someone took those keys and put them to use," Deputy Kinkaid said, likely working an extra-long shift that day.

"Yeah, it seems that way, doesn't it?"

Bridgette rolled her eyes toward Griffin and turned her attention to me. Griffin and Logan set about searching the surroundings outside the duplex. Kinkaid greeted the guys with a nod of familiarity.

"Don't touch anything, fellas," the deputy shouted after them. They both nodded their heads. Turning his attention back to me, he asked, "Did you notice anything missing?"

"Not that I've noticed so far. Just ransacking the place. Just like the store, nothing seems missing. Right now, it just seems I'm being terrorized."

The deputy took some notes, and his partner looked around. Nothing seemed to warrant the crime lab coming, but his partner took photos.

"I think you should be staying with someone else tonight. You have a place to go?" He turned his attention to Bridgette, like he was instructing her to invite me. If it wasn't such a tense situation, I might have laughed.

"I'm not going anywhere, thanks. This is my home. But, someone should check on Jessica next door. If the intruder wants to come back and face me or her, they'll have to come face us in person. Tomorrow, Joe is coming to help me change all the locks, so, I'll just be staying home tonight."

"I'll stay with her," Logan said. It was a statement instead of a suggestion, so I knew there was no arguing with him: but it made me nervous.

I looked to my other friends, unsure of what do to. I knew Griffin had to leave early the next morning, but I wasn't sure about this. Logan was so sure, though, arguing didn't seem like an option. And, his skills might come in handy if someone came back.

"I'll be staying, too," Bridgette said. Thank God for my best friend.

Deputy Kinkaid looked around the room, and satisfied I'd be taken care of, he tipped his hat. After telling us they'd be in touch, he and his partner left us to clean up the mess.

"I'll take Bridgette to get her stuff. Logan, can I stop by your place and grab some things? I'll check on Jessi on the way out, and then we'll be back." Griffin sprang into problem solving mode.

Bridgette and Griffin left leaving Logan and me alone in my living room. He started looking around, looked out the sliding door, and moved toward the kitchen.

"What do you think they were looking for?" He asked.

"I honestly don't know. I mean, a break in at the store could make sense if they'd taken anything - but my money, my inventory? It was all accounted for. I'm not wealthy. I don't have anything here worth stealing, and again, nothing missing as far as I can tell. Other than my spare keys."

I collapsed on the couch. I watched Logan work his way around the room. He turned back toward me from the kitchen.

"Is it possible you could have other family wealth that you don't know about? Like, maybe from time past?" he asked, almost as if he knew something I didn't. I saw wheels turning in his head, and my senses fired.

"I really doubt it." I said.

The only money we had in the family mostly came from the sale of my grandparents shop across the water and was split between my parents and me. I used my portion to put my down payment toward my own shop.

"I mean, maybe your parents or grandparents didn't even know about it." He wasn't really speaking to me anymore. It seemed more like he was trying to work something out in his head. He turned and under his breath said, "or maybe it's someone else and your family is being mistaken for them."

I shifted on the couch, feeling more than a little shaken and confused. He really seemed to already have an idea, but still hadn't shared much about who he was or why he was here.

"Ok, what do you know?" I asked, trying to keep my voice even. "Why does it seem like you've got a big puzzle you're trying to put together? Why are you even here doing what you're doing? If you expect trust around here, we need the truth; need to know who you are."

Logan sighed. He couldn't keep his story to himself forever, and he knew it. "I was a cop, about to make detective. One of the youngest in our precinct to pass the exam and make it, but some things happened. I decided it was time to go back to journalism. I was working as an investigative journalist for an online paper. I wasn't there long when I was lured into a setup, still don't know by who, and I'm pretty sure they wanted me dead."

Logan paused and turned back to me. His face showed little emotion, but his tone made me realize it was harder sharing his story than he thought. I tried to keep my face straight, not wanting to keep him from sharing. But, my heart hurt just knowing he'd come that close to death. The thought gutted me. Unfortunately, these high stress situations forced everyone to learn things about each other we weren't ready to share.

" They got the next best thing. The blow to my head cost me most of my eye-sight and I walked away from the job. It was a lot of healing and physical therapy. I didn't know what I wanted to do. So, I started re-learning. Everything.

I've spent the last three years figuring out life as a partially blind man and learning how to be a detective again. I passed my private detective license exam and came here to open up shop for practice."

"Here? But why here? Just because of what happened last winter?" I asked, unsure why any private investigator would want to move to a town with virtually no crime.

"I've read the statistics. I knew in this town it would mostly be petty stuff I could get my feet wet with. Even after the fires, I didn't think there would be two major break-ins right when I got to town. I swear, I had nothing to do with them, and that's the truth."

" I believe you about that, but you do seem to know something." I could tell by what he'd said earlier, he was on to something. "Something that has to do with money. And maybe my parents or grandparents?"

" I did some digging, used my old resources. Your family, or a family with a similar name, did have a fortune. A fairly sizable one. But, I'm not sure what happened to a large portion of it or where it is now. No one knows, it just disappeared. But a key to that may be just what our break-in friend is looking for. Someone who thinks it is your family and you have access to it somehow."

I looked at the damage all around me. I couldn't picture anyone in my family having the kind of money that would prompt this kind of destruction. I was simply at a loss.

"But, we don't have money. At least, not on my dad's side." I plopped back on the couch, and Logan joined me. Close enough for comfort, but not too close.

"What about your mom's side?" he asked gently.

"I don't know much. My great-grandma didn't have much of a relationship with my grandma. And, I think she was estranged from her family. My grandma was nice enough, but my mom wasn't close to her, either, so neither was I. But, I haven't ever heard of any family money. The only things we have from them are a couple of journals and a painting."

"A painting?" Hope piqued his voice.

"Yeah, my great-grandma was an artist. We have one of her pieces left that's been passed down. It's hanging in the hallway there between the bedrooms."

"That doesn't sound like something someone would be after then," Logan sounded defeated. I really wanted nothing more than to hold his hand in mine to offer us both a little comfort, but I'd never do that. It was so outside the bounds of any professional relationship, which this was clearly turning out to be.

My thoughts were interrupted by a knock at the door. Logan got up, looked through the peep hole, and then let Griffin and Bridgette back in. Ben followed close behind with enough food for all of us and left after Griffin paid him.

"Okay, I wish I could stay too, Kass," Griffin said after we ate, "but I gotta be up and out early to head to Portland. You're in good hands here, though, so I know I can go without worry."

I nodded and walked him out, giving him a hug before he left. I locked the door behind him, and then for good measure, I double checked the sliding patio door. The plans for a book and bath long forgotten, I spent the rest of the evening chatting with my friends before exhaustion took over.

CHAPTER 6

MY ALARM WENT OFF too early the next morning. I rolled over and faced the wall. Though my friends had stayed over to help me, none of us really did any cleaning up the night before. There was still a lot of work to be done. I knew I had to meet Joe at the store, but I couldn't drag myself out of bed to do so.

Grabbing my phone out of instinct, I noticed a missed text.

LOGAN: GOOD MORNING. HOPE YOU GOT SOME SLEEP. HAD TO LEAVE EARLY. I'LL CHECK ON YOU LATER.

My heart skipped a beat and a smile played on my lips. Before I could send a response, a soft knock on the door interrupted my thoughts.

"Kass, you up?" Bridgette attempted a whisper. Whispering simply wasn't her strong suit, and it made me chuckle to hear her try.

"Yeah, I'm awake. Come on in." I tried to sit up, but my body refused.

"Hey, I brought you some coffee. Griffin called on his way to that news story down in Portland; he'll be back in a day or so. Everything is all safe out there, but it's just me and you. Logan left earlier, left a note"

I nodded, taking the mug from my friend and immediately setting it on the nightstand. "Yeah, he sent a text too. As for Griffin, my money is on stopping in Seattle to see Shiloh, so, probably a couple of days." We both laughed. "I need to call Joe, and have him come here first, I think."

"Already done. Griffin called him last night. He'll be here in about 20 minutes to change your locks, and Jessi's too, just to be safe. I'm going to go with Joe to the store while they install the new windows, door, and locks there. Then, I'll just take care of the getting the store in order for however long you need. You stay here and get things back in order here. I figured Logan wouldn't mind coming back this morning. I'm sure he'll make sure you're not alone."

"You all don't need to do that. Really. But, thank you." I finally willed myself to sit up and look around my bedroom. The mess from the night before greeted and overwhelmed me. I took a sip of the coffee, knowing, once again, my friends knew me better than I knew myself.

"We know we don't have to, but, we're going to anyway." Bridgette winked at me, eliciting the desired cringe. "So, how are we going to find out what's going on. What could they possibly be looking for?"

"I honestly don't know. Logan has a theory, though..." I let the sentence fall, not sure if I should tell Bridgette what Logan had discovered.

"And, what is it?" Bridgette lifted her eyebrow and pursed her lips. If anyone had news in the town, it was her. Not being in the know didn't sit well with her.

"He thinks my family could have had some money that disappeared somewhere along the way. Or a family with a similar name did? I don't know. The money just disappeared somewhere along the way. Like, vanished. No trace. Logan has this idea that the person doing all this is looking for a key to all that or information about it. Isn't that crazy?" I looked to her for confirmation, which was met with excitement.

"No, that's brilliant. That's why nothing has been missing. They've been looking for something specific, something that will lead to a big payoff; and somehow they think you have it." I could see the wheels in Bridgette's head turning, trying to figure out the mystery. "We have to find it before they do."

"Find what? That shop is basically all I own. We don't have money. I don't have many cousins, at least not on my dad's side, and none on my mom's side. Everything following my grandma's death was civil. My parents & aunt got what they wanted. There's no money here. So, why not take the money from the safe or the register?"

"Maybe the family fortune is bigger than you know. And maybe, they are after that specifically," Bridgette wondered.

"That doesn't make any sense to me. Why risk all of that, but not take the easy money. It was right there. I mean, sure, not a lot of money, but still, after all that, it was easy money. Money in the safe. Money in the register. Even my stash in the freezer is still there."

"I doubt they checked your freezer, Kass. Why would they do that?" Bridgette wrinkled her nose. She always thought it was strange that I kept some valuables in my freezer.

"I don't know. I know you think it's weird, but it's, like, a known hiding place for valuables. I'm pretty sure I got that idea from a movie or book or something. But, no, it's all still there." I shook my head and ran my fingers through the tendrils that had fallen from my day old messy bun.

"I'm fairly sure you're the only one who would take advice like that from a movie, so I'm not surprised your freezer stash is still there. As for the store, I bet Logan's right, and they're just looking for something they think is bigger or more important. And, we're going to figure out what it is."

I knew once Bridgette got a hold of a good idea, she wouldn't let go. My only choice was to get on board, or I'd just be dragged along for the ride. Something I definitely didn't want.

A knock at the door startled both of us, and Bridgette let out a squeal. "I'll get it," she said. "I bet it's Joe here to fix the door."

I nodded, watching my best friend leave. Before doing anything else, I texted Logan back.

KASSIDY: SO, YOU PLAN TO COME BACK AND CHECK ON ME TODAY?

LOGAN: YUP, I'LL BE BACK AT YOUR PLACE WITHIN THE HOUR. I PLAN TO STICK CLOSE UNTIL

WE FIGURE THIS ALL OUT. CAN'T HAVE YOU GET YOURSELF HURT, SWEETS.

Oh, my heart. He called me sweets. And, I was all about it.

KASSIDY: I WON'T ARGUE WITH THAT. WILL YOU HELP ME GET MY HOUSE IN ORDER TODAY?

LOGAN: WHATEVER YOU NEED, SWEETS

I'd do whatever I needed to do to keep him calling me that. That term of endearment had my head swimming, and I couldn't help but wonder what it would be like to hear it coming from his mouth, in his voice. I could almost hear it in my head.

After another minute of day dreaming, I got up to get clothes on. I opted for something comfortable, since I was in for a day of cleaning and organizing my usually spotless apartment. Right now, it resembled something more like Bridgette's apartment, messy and scattered.

"Hi Joe," I greeted as I joined him and Bridgette in the living room.

"Kassidy, I'm so sorry about all this. I was just telling Bridgette here you need a security system, with some cameras, and maybe a few more heavy duty locks." Joe nodded, as if he'd already decided this for himself.

"That's ok, Joe, just a new knob and lock will work for today. They won't be able to use any of the keys they got. The only other key on the ring goes to something I don't even remember now. I think my grandparents' old storage we cleared out or something."

"Maybe that's what the thief is after." Bridgette snapped her fingers.

"But, then, why break in here? They had the key," I pointed out.

"Maybe they needed the address to what the key opened, and they thought you'd have it here. That's why they didn't touch your freezer stash."

Joe shook his head at our musings. "Well, I still think you need a high tech system here, but I'm getting those new locks put on right now. I've got a guy next door working on Jessica's locks, too, just in case. Then, I'll head to the store and take care of those locks, doors, and windows.

Your metal grate system will be here in a few days, and I'll work with a team to get that going, too."

"Can I get you some coffee or something Joe?" I asked, trying to play host, even in the middle of a mess.

"No thanks, already had two cups today. I'll just get started here," he said.

He set to work on the door, leaving Bridgette and me to continue our guesses about what the thief was after. We spent the next few minutes beginning to reorganize the kitchen.

"All done," Joe said, placing a set of keys on the counter.

"I've got three keys here. Two for you, and one for your parents. I think instead of keeping that spare you've got in the store, you need to give it to someone else. A safe person. Bridgette, maybe. Or that Jessica girl next door." Joe handed the keys to me.

"One might go to her or Jessica, I guess," I said. "I don't know Jessi too well yet. But since she's right next door, it might not be a bad idea to exchange new keys with her."

Bridgette and Joe both expressed their agreement.

"I'll head over to the store now. Will one of you be coming over there with me? I think you can open back up, our work shouldn't bother business too much."

"I'm going," Bridgette said. "Could I catch a ride with you, Joe?"

Joe nodded and turned to gather his tools. After a quick hug, Bridgette grabbed her purse and followed Joe out the door. I closed it behind them, and ensured both locks were secure before turning to face my mess of an apartment again.

CHAPTER 7

A KNOCK AT THE door caused me to jump, breaking my concentration as I tried, and failed, to focus on organizing my living room. I looked through the peep hole to see Logan's face. My heart fluttered at the sight of him.

I carefully opened the door, looking around as I let him in. I sighed a breath of relief when I was able to close the door behind him. If he hadn't already seen the house in disarray, I would be extremely embarrassed to have him in with the way it looked now.

"How are you doing?" he asked, taking a seat on the sofa.

"I don't know. As good as I can be, I guess. Thanks for coming back to hang out with me today. I'm sure you had better things to do."

"Than hang out with the most interesting girl in town? I don't think so." There was teasing in his voice that softened his demeanor.

"And, what would make me the most interesting girl in town? Because someone keeps breaking into my spaces?" I tried to match his teasing, but instead my tone sounded self-deprecating. Considering how little time we'd actually had to get to know one another, I wasn't sure why he would find me interesting.

"That, and you just seem like an interesting person. The extra drama? That's just a bonus." He winked again, reminding me to tell him sometime that I hate it when people wink.

"So, how are your cases going? I mean, you did say you were working on cases, right? I thought you'd said something yesterday before everything went a bit crazy."

"I wrapped a case up this morning. I'm doing some research for you, but now the only other case I'm on is my own. Neither case is moving forward at the moment. Do you have any new ideas regarding your case since last night?"

Logan got up to move around the space, checking everything slowly, almost as if he was looking for something specific. He checked under furniture and pictures on the wall. He even looked into boxes and my fake plants.

"No, we don't. Uh, Logan, what are you doing?"

"Just checking for bugs," he said like it was the most ordinary and obvious thing in the world.

"Bugs? Like, spiders and stuff?"

He looked at me like I'd just grown two heads. "No, bugs, like listening devices. Like, for someone who may be spying on you. I forgot to do that last night, so I'm doing it now."

"You think someone's spying on me?"

"I really don't know, but you can't be too careful. They are going to a lot of trouble to find something. If they think you know what it is or where it is, they might try to listen to see if you bring it up." He shrugged and kept looking.

I should have returned to my cleaning, but instead I watched him as he moved through the living area and into the kitchen. He was extremely thorough with everything. Once he was finished with the main rooms, he looked back at me.

"Okay if I go back to the two bedrooms? Just to be safe?"

Something about the way he stopped to ask permission while he was so focused on his task was very endearing. "Sure, go ahead."

My phone vibrated in my pocket. *DAD*. I braced myself. "Hi Dad, what's up?"

I tried to keep my voice steady, knowing he already knew what was going on. Too many people in this town knew my parents for this not to be an issue. Also, they own the duplex, I reminded myself.

"Kass, what's going on out there? Are you okay? Why didn't you call us?" Dad bombarded me with questions, and I secretly wished Logan would come back out so I could excuse myself from the phone call.

"Dad, it's fine. Joe is taking care of things at the store as we speak. The locks have already been changed here. I'll make sure you get a copy of the new keys. Everything's fine. Honest."

"From what everyone says it doesn't sound fine. You should have called us."

"You're right, I know. But, it's been crazy. I would have called later today, though, because I do need you to come out and look at the security system you put in at the shop. Somehow, it was disabled. I don't know how they did that."

"Okay, Kassy-bean, I'll come out tomorrow to take a look at the shop. We have an important job I have to be on site for today. I will make sure we install something even more secure next. And, as soon as we can, we'll get to the house, too. But, if anything like this happens again, especially at your home, you call us immediately. Got it?"

"Of course, Dad. I got it."

"Mom and I love you very much, you know that, right Kassy-bean?"

"I know Dad. I love you, too. I need to get back to cleaning. Bye, Dad."

Logan came back in just as I hung up with my dad.

"Find anything?" I asked, turning my attention to the tasks in front of me.

"Not really. Doesn't seem like they've left anything behind. Which, I think is a good thing." He paused, rubbing the back of his neck with his hand. "I overheard you talking to your dad. You didn't tell your parents what happened?"

"No, I got so caught up in everything and trying to figure it all out I just didn't yet."

"You're lucky you just got a phone call. My parents live on the other side of the country, but my mom would have shown up on my doorstep as soon as she heard."

"Yeah, I'm kind of surprised she's not here. I'm guessing Dad talked her out of it by promising to call. If I know her, she was at the job site making sure he called."

We stood there awkwardly, neither knowing what to say next. I knew he was here to help me clean and make sure I wasn't alone; but asking him to help me clean the house wasn't something I felt super comfortable with.

Logan was the one to finally break the awkward silence. "What can I do to help? Put me to work." He rubbed his hands together before leaning on the back of the couch. The gesture pulled his clean t-shirt tight across his chest and arms. I tried not to focus on the man with all the lean muscles leaning over my couch.

"Well, most of the books and stuff were taken off the shelves in the office, could you start putting those back? They don't need to be perfect or in a particular way for now, just off the floor and in some kind of order would be good."

"I can do that."

"Can I get you water or coffee or anything? Are you hungry? You left so early this morning. I mean, I don't really have a lot in the way of food at the moment, but I could scrounge up something," I offered.

I hated having company over in the middle of a mess with nothing to offer. My mom taught me to be a much better host than that, but I was doing the best I could with what I had.

"I'm not hungry, but coffee would be great." He smiled. The hostess in me was relieved to have something to offer.

"Go ahead and get started in the other room, I'll bring you the coffee."

I set about making us both a warm cup of coffee, bringing his back to the small home office I'd made out of the second bedroom. He was already practically finished cleaning up in there.

By lunchtime, we had the house in basic order once again. It wasn't exactly back in order to my standards, but good enough, so we headed out for lunch. I knew when we came back that afternoon, I'd need to go visit Jessi and exchange our new keys. We'd both need to make sure there was a copy available to my parents, who were technically our landlords. Talking with Jessi about this whole mess was not something I was looking forward to.

The pub was actually fairly empty when we arrived. We sat in the back corner booth, the one my friends and I thought of as "our booth" Even though it was a fairly large, round booth, Logan scooted close to me. Odd as it was, I really wanted him to put his arm around me.

After we got our order in, we settled back in place. Suddenly, our booth was filled with several younger, questioning faces as Dark Autumn infiltrated our space. Dark Autumn was the band Sebastian, Ben, and Olivia had formed, and Persephone was mixing music and producing for them.

Persephone, with her long, dark hair and purple streaks spoke first, "Kass, we're so sorry for everything that's been happening. It's like another nightmare. Are you okay?"

I noticed her eyes were marked with darkness. She'd been through some things, and now it seems the break ins were shaking her up. I hated that I was adding to her pain.

"Thanks, guys. Have you met Logan?" I gestured to him, and they all shook their heads. I introduced him to Persephone and Sebastian, a brooding guy with dirty blonde hair. He grunted a hello. Ben, a guy who couldn't keep a smile off his face greeted Logan with a handshake. And, last was Olivia, the girl with blue hair that I'm sure he'd seen working different jobs around town.

"Nice to meet you all." Recognizing Persephone's name from all the stories of the fire and loss of her grandparents, he said, "Persephone, I heard about what happened in December. I'm so sorry for your loss."

She sucked in a sharp breath. She gave a sad smile and said, "thank you."

"What are you all up to this afternoon?" I asked them.

"Well, uh," Ben started, "we know this is terrible timing and all, but we wanted to ask you..."

Ben let his words fall. I knew Ben. He was one of those guys who just always wanted people to be happy. He brought the happy with him anywhere he went. Whatever they wanted to ask, he clearly didn't want to pile more onto my plate.

"We know this isn't great timing," Olivia continued where Ben left off, "we have the opportunity to shoot a music video with a production group Perse works with. They want to come out in a week or two. If we push it out a couple weeks, we were hoping we could shoot some scenes in The Bookshop. We know it has to be cleaned up and things are crazy now, but we were hoping. The opportunity just kind of fell in our laps."

"Guys that's amazing. Of course, you can film in the shop. I'd be glad to let you do that. Maybe the shop will get famous, and I'll get lots of new customers."

I couldn't help but smile. I loved being able to help my friends realize their dreams. A professional music video would be great for these guys.

"Thank you so much," Olivia gushed. The guys offered their thanks too. Persephone just gave another sad smile.

"Now, if only we could find someone to be on keys, we'd be in a much better place," Sebastian finally spoke, but he was looking directly at Persephone.

"Not gonna happen, Sebbie, already told you. I just mix. That's all." Though her words were negative, it was the first time since they'd sat down that I saw a hint of happiness dance in her eyes. I had a feeling I knew why when I looked at his face.

"Too bad my sister doesn't live around here. She plays the piano. She was in a band on keys for a while in college. Lani would love you guys, I'm sure," Logan said.

"So, can you convince her to move here? Like, tomorrow?" Ben asked, sounding a little too eager.

Logan brushed it off with a laugh, "probably not. She just got a new job she seems to really like out in South Carolina. As much as she misses me, I don't think it's enough to make her move here."

"Bummer, we really could use a fourth."

After a bit more conversation, they left, and Logan and I ate our food. I didn't want lunch to end too soon, because going back meant facing Jessi, the woman next door. I really worried about how she would react to everything.

I opted to go talk to Jessi alone, so I left Logan to just settle in at my place to wait. I noticed him choose the chair on my front porch before I headed over to face Jessi.

CHAPTER 8

I HELD MY BREATH, unsure whether I wanted Jessi to be home or not. I hated letting this new tenant know something so dangerous had happened in the duplex, but I also wanted to get the key to her as soon as possible.

"Kassidy," Jessi flung the door open and threw her arms around me. "I heard what happened. I'm so sorry. Thanks for having my locks changed. Are you okay?"

"Yeah, I am, but my place wasn't."

Jessi led me into the living room, which also seemed to serve as her home office. The furniture resembled more of an office lounge rather than someone's living room. Jessi said that was so her clients would feel more comfortable coming to talk to her, instead of feeling like they were invading her home. Jessi's desk was in one corner, and the rest of the space was situated with a couch and several stuffed chairs around a small coffee table. One end table was situated between the sofa and an angled chair. A mini fridge with a coffee bar on top was situated between the desk and a small portable electric fireplace.

"Can I get you anything?" Jessi asked, opening the fridge and grabbing a water.

"No thanks. I won't be long. I just came over to tell you about the incident and thank you for letting Joe's guy change your lock. Oh, and see if you wanted to exchange keys."

"Man, so scary the thief had a key." Jessi grew pale.

"It's so weird. They took my spare keys from the store. And, they definitely used the key to get in. So, to be safe we changed the locks. Here you go." I set the key on the small coffee table in front of us.

"Thank you. How crazy this all is. I'm so sorry this is happening. I'm surprised you even thought to bring a key over here." Jessi grabbed one of her new keys and handed it to me.

"I'll get this to my parents. They'll need a copy of each of them," I shrugged as Jessi picked up my new key. I stared blankly at the space the key had just been.

"Is anything else missing? From here or the store? I mean, I heard the store was broken into, too. Did they take anything?" Jessi stuck the new keys in one of her desk drawers.

"No, not that we can figure. Nothing but my spare keys. Which, I don't know why they would even do that. Those keys do nothing. They obviously found a way into the store without the keys, and the only other keys there were to my house, which now don't work, and some other small key that literally leads to nowhere."

"Nowhere? Are you sure?" Jessi was intrigued, just like everyone else seemed to be.

"I'm pretty sure. I'm pretty sure the only key left was the small key to the storage we cleared out when my grandparents died. Nothing else is in there. So, it really is to nowhere. To nothing."

"Wow. Why would someone want random keys then?" Jessi settled into one of her overstuffed chairs.

"I wish we knew, Jessi. I really do. I don't have money, contrary to what people might think. My grandparents did ok, but they weren't wealthy. Neither are my parents. I honestly have no idea why the only thing someone would take would be keys."

"Maybe there's something more pressing to them?" Jessi asked.

"Yeah, Logan and Bridgette said the same thing. But, what that would be, no one knows. Logan has a guess, though."

"Logan? Has a guess?" Jessi repeated. She looked a little concerned. "Remind me who Logan is again."

"He's new in town," I waved away like swatting a fly. "A PI who came here for some peace and quiet. He has theories. I don't think I believe them, though."

"Wow, a PI right here in Miller's Pointe. Who woulda thought. Nothing ever happens here. Well, until the last few months, I guess. Maybe he brought em with him." Jessi finally opened the water bottle she'd been shuffling around and took a drink.

"Look, Jessi, I don't want to be rude, but I have a lot of stuff to get back in order. The intruder left me a mess and a half, and I won't be able to properly rest until it's all cleaned up and perfectly sorted."

"You do like things organized, don't you?" "Yeah, just how I am, I guess."

Jessi led me to the door, where we said our goodbyes. Jessi promised to keep an eye out for anything suspicious and thanked me for the key exchange.

For some reason, my meeting with Jessi left me feeling more vulnerable and violated than I'd realized. I headed back for what little mess was left in my apartment, hoping by organizing everything again, I'd begin to feel safe and at peace again. Like I always had before.

Logan was waiting on my porch when I finished with Jessi. Even though I'd thought he would stay, I still found myself surprised.

"You stayed?" I asked. Part of me hoped he stayed for more than just because he wanted answers. I hoped he stayed because he wanted spend more time with me.

"Didn't know how that would go, and you can't be too careful. Can I stay and help with anything else?"

"I don't know if there's much else left; but, you're welcome to stay. If I'm being honest, I'm not sure I'm quite ready to be alone."

I opened the door and moved aside for him to join me inside. He settled on the couch. My nervous energy wouldn't allow me to sit.

"Can I get you water or something?" I offered. I was already moving toward the kitchen to get a bottle of water and grabbed two, just in case.

"Water is just fine. So, where do we start with phase two?" He took the water bottle I held out.

"Phase two?" I asked before taking a sip of my own water.

"Yeah, earlier, you just wanted us to get things put away, but not organized. I have a feeling you want to get it all organized again a certain way. The way you like it."

"I don't know what you're talking about," I lied, trying to convince him. How had he already figured out how important having my space organized was for me? I didn't want him to think I was a freak, even though I was when it came to organizing my space.

"So, if we just sit here and talk, you'll be able to relax?" he asked, settling in on the couch. He patted the spot next to him, as if it was a challenge.

"Sure," I said, sitting on the edge of my comfy chair instead of next to him. It took barely ten seconds of silence to send me out of my chair. "Okay, I can't handle it. I want to get it back how it was."

Logan let out a hearty laugh, which warmed my heart. "I thought that might be the case, so where do we start?"

"Well, we can start in here and work our way through, though I don't know how much you'll actually be able to do."

"How about this, you start the organizing, and I'll do some research to see if we can get this puzzle solved."

"Okay, great. Let's do it."

I was glad for the company, even if I didn't have work for him to do. I was happy to have him just sitting in my living room looking for answers to my case while I put order back in my world. I wanted to work quickly so I could just sit with him and enjoy his company like we'd done at lunch.

Starting with the living room, I began reorganizing my home; what was once supposed to be my safe space. Near the front door was a small vanity that I used as both a vanity and an entrance table. I started with that space, the drawer having been taken out and its contents dumped. Earlier, I'd just put everything back in, now I relished the ability to put it back in place properly. Something about seeing everything back where it belonged brought me peace.

I worked counterclockwise around the living room, straightening the curtains to the sliding door to the left of the entry desk. The sliding door led to the back patio. I was pleasantly surprised the curtains were still mostly on the rod. A knock on the door interrupted my straightening the fake Ficus I kept in the corner by the vanity.

"Be right back, Betty," I said to the Ficus, which Bridgette had named Betty when we found it by the side of the road.

"Betty?" Logan asked, looking up.

"Bridgette named her." I shrugged as he followed me to the door. I smiled knowing he wasn't letting me do any of this on my own.

A glance through the peep hole revealed a delivery guy on the other side of the door. I opened it for him and took my package, no doubt some more books I'd ordered for my house or the store. I couldn't quite remember. Logan watched the entire time, keeping an eye out to make sure nothing happened.

I got back to work in the living room, and Logan settled back in with his phone for more research. "Has there been a lot of crime in this town before?" Logan asked.

"Not really," I answered, starting to get my kitchen back in order. "I mean, a few years ago, the basketball team got in some trouble for stealing the mascot statue from a neighboring town in retaliation for the other town stealing ours. You know, sports rivalry and all. But, big crime? Like what's been happening lately? No, not really. Not until last December, you know."

"It's strange it would start now. Do you happen to know if there's anything in the town's history? Perhaps way back?"

"Bridgette told me about the possible money stuff with the Gideons and some others. Honestly, history isn't my thing. If you want history, you want Griffin. His family was one of the founding families here in town, plus they have access to all the newspaper archives. He's who you'll want to talk to about that."

I moved from cupboard to cupboard trying to get everything exactly as it had been before, but not sure I could even remember at this point. There was so much going on in my head. And, all I wanted to be doing was sitting on the couch with the handsome man asking all the questions. I just couldn't do it until order was back in my life.

Logan nodded in understanding and continued focusing on the phone in front of him. I couldn't help wonder if he wanted me to be in there with him as much as I wanted to be.

"Also," I continued, "I can probably help you dig up history about the town and try to find possible connections. I'm really good at researching and my family has been a part of this town almost since the beginning."

Logan moved toward the island that separated the kitchen from the main space, "So, you are the one I should talk to about town history?"

I looked at him quizzically; then, said, "I mean, some of it, I guess."

"So, like, what, you can be the one to help me dig up the town's dirt and connections and family drama and things like that?" He smiled at me, his blue eyes brightening. As if that was possible.

"I guess so. I mean, yes. Like I said, I'm good at research, and my family has been a part of the town for a long time.

Griffin's family helped found the town, though, so they have the in there. Like I said, archives and all. But, also, Bud and Mabel's families helped out, so Bridgette might be another avenue where we could get information, especially if you want town drama and gossip. But, what does town gossip and drama have to do with the break ins?"

"Honestly, maybe nothing, but knowing patterns in the town could help. If nothing else, maybe help me know what I'm in for around here. Also, knowing if this person is attacking the town or you personally."

"Pretty sure this is personal." I wiped a stray tear from my cheek. They'd been falling every so often since the big break in at the store, no matter how much I tried to stop them.

"I know it seems they are after you personally. I'm just looking into all possible angles. We're going to get to the bottom of this; we just need to look at everything."

Logan reached out and rested his hand on mine, which had stopped midway through wiping down the island. I resisted the urge to pull away as energy coursed between us. I knew at that moment I better be careful around this man.

"Have you found out if anything was missing so far?" He asked.

"No, nothing's missing. It doesn't make any sense to me. Why would someone attempt to break in three times and not take anything but those keys? Not any of the money, no inventory. No jewelry Nothing at all as far as I can see. No note to explain. Not trying to do it while I'm there, so not "after me", after me. I honestly don't know."

"Usually, all those signs point to them looking for something specific. There is something they have in mind that they are after, and it's not really you. I'll head to the office and do more research a little later. We don't have a lot to go on, so it's tricky. I know it really bothered you before, but could I look into your history as well, Kassidy?" Logan didn't call me Kass like everyone else did, which I was so thankful for.

"Sure. You've got my permission to look into my history, my family history, the history of the store, my grandparents' store. Whatever you think you'll need. I'll give you any information. I just want to start getting some answers to all of this."

Logan nodded, and he returned to the main room to keep researching while I kept organizing. By five, everything was just as neat and orderly as it had been, as if nothing terrible had happened just the day before.

I got us more drinks and messaged Bridgette to finish up at the store and join us. If Logan and Bridgette were so keen on sleuthing, I would join them. After all, my livelihood now seemed to depend on it.

CHAPTER 9

BRIDGETTE ARRIVED AROUND 6:00 p.m. with some food from the pub and settled in on the couch between Logan and me. "So, what do we know? And what do we need to know?"

"First things first, how are things at the store?" I asked her. I hated leaving someone else in charge of putting things at the store back together, even someone who knows it as well as I do, like Bridgette. It's still my baby, the place I used all of my inheritance to invest in, that I was barely hanging on to. I really hoped to get back open as soon as possible.

"I had Olivia come in for a while to help. One more day, and we might have most of the things back in order to get back open, at least for most sections and the lounge and writing stations. The coffee station is completely destroyed. We'll have to go to the mainland to pick up new coffee equipment, unless you want to wait for it to ship."

Bridgette had a knack for saying things off hand, as if just speaking about the most mundane things. I both appreciated and hated that quality of hers. Yet even this moment helped me feel just a little more at ease.

"No, we better go get some stuff from the store. Maybe we can go tomorrow. It's not our biggest draw, but it's still helpful and expected by now. Though, I'm not sure where the money for it will come from."

"I'll buy them and donate, just like I did the others. No big deal." Bridgette shrugged, as if she was just talking about lending me a sweater, and not buying my entire coffee station needs. Again.

"If you insist," was all I could think to say. I knew her well enough to know arguing was going to do me no good.

"So, your dad's last name is Winters, right?" Logan asked, abruptly pulling Bridgette and I away from shop talk. "What about your mom's maiden name?"

"Uh, her maiden name is Smith. Nice and generic, right?" I said, as he typed something into his phone.

"What about her mother's maiden name?" He asked.

"Um, I think it was Blackwell or Blackburn or something like that. I'd have to ask my mom."

Logan typed more into his phone. His face held a tight look of concentration, and it was clear he was trying to figure something out. Bridgette and I both watched him for a minute before either of us spoke.

"What did you guys get done today or find out today?" Bridgette asked, taking a bite of a chip.

"We got everything put back in order and discussed some possibilities about the family. I really just have no idea what is going on, and I don't understand why they'd target me. This place - and the store - are supposed to be my safe places. That's gone now. What do I do?"

I leaned my head on Bridgette's shoulder as she chomped on the chips and salsa she'd brought us. She held a chip dipped in salsa to me, with the silent command to eat. I took the chip and ate it, not lifting my head from her shoulder. Logan sat continuing to look at things on his phone.

"And, what are you doing over there?" Bridgette asked Logan, pushing some food toward him on the coffee table.

"I'm looking for possibilities related to Kassidy's mom's family. She knows so much about her dad's family, but I think the answers come from her mom's line, if it's family related."

Bridgette nodded in understanding, not disrupting my head. Somehow, she and I always knew what the other one needed, and we always came through. Just like she was doing right now.

"Does your mom know much about her family?" Logan asked.

"I don't know," I sighed, lifting my head. He had looked away from his phone, so I met his eyes. "We had some old paintings that had been passed down, and I think a journal or two from somewhere down the line in her family. But most of the written family records I have come from Dad's family."

I finally decided to eat some of the food in front of me. The burger I got was perfect, as all Bud's burgers were. Clearly, Bridgette had told him it was for me, because it was a Kassidy special: well-done with no onions and extra pickles and a special mayo-ketchup sauce.

"Did you talk to Jessi at all today? What does she have to say about all this?" Bridgette asked, her mouth full of her own veggie burger.

"I don't know. She didn't seem too concerned. Just asked a lot of questions, so more confused than anything. Worried for me, I guess."

Logan finally put his phone down long enough to devour his burger, which took all of a couple minutes, and he was back to his phone.

"What kinds of paintings were handed down?" He asked.

"I don't know, some stuff my great-grandma painted. She was kind of a bohemian, artistic spirit, from what I hear. She left a few of her completed works behind, and the rest were just trashed or something, I guess."

"So, nothing fancy or expensive?" He asked. I could almost see the wheels turning in his head.

"No, nothing like that. From what my mom knows, there wasn't much money in her family. And, there wasn't a lot of family in her family. Her grandma was a simple, and private person. She kept to herself. And, my grandma kind of went her own way, and so did my mom and my Aunt Susan. None of them were ever that close, and there was only one daughter in each generation, except my mom's. So, there's really nothing there that I can think of."

"Well, that seems like a bust," Bridgette said, gathering everyone's trash. "So, tomorrow, what time should we get started on the store? I have to be in the bar for the dinner crowd."

"Let's just work a few hours tomorrow, maybe twelve to three? That way you can start your usual four p.m. shift at

Brew & Bake. We'll finish it off the next day, and then I'll reopen the day after, whatever of the store that I can."

"Sounds good," Bridgette said from the kitchen where she'd just thrown out the trash. She then gathered the trash and sealed off the trash bag. "I need to get to the bar now, actually, for the late crowd. Bud doesn't have another bar tender tonight. I'll take this trash out."

I nodded and waved goodbye as she left. Turning my attention to Logan, I asked, "so, what do you think?"

"Hm, I honestly am not too sure. There's a lot more research that needs to be done. Do you think you can look through some of that written family history of your dad's family you were talking about?"

"Sure, I can do that soon."

"Okay, I'll keep following other leads as well. You okay here? Do you want someone to stay the night again? I'm not sure if I'm comfortable with you being alone after all this, especially without a security system here," he stretched, unsure if he should get up to leave.

"I'm fine. I promise. If anything goes wrong I'll call you. I'll see you later. Thanks for helping today."

I walked Logan to the door and made sure to lock it behind him. Turning back into my house, I checked every door and window before settling in for the night. I opted for a night in bed with a book to the couch and tv, feeling like I could lock myself in my room if need be. A couple hours later, I fell into a dreamless sleep.

CHAPTER 10

9 A.M. SHOOT.

I crashed last night after my friends left.

After getting some coffee, I returned to my bed. Now, I was ready to search for more answers.

Before I went looking for any, though, I checked my phone out of habit. Logan's name lit up the lock screen with a few messages.

LOGAN: GOOD MORNING, SWEETS.

LOGAN: LET ME KNOW HOW I CAN HELP TODAY. I'LL BE AROUND.

Oh, my heart. There he went again, calling me Sweets. I really wished I could think of a way to help him today, more because I wanted to see him than anything.

In my newly organized room, I pulled a box out from under my bed. It seemed the intruder missed this box. Lifting the lid, I studied all the leather bound books inside. I pulled out one of my grandmother's diaries, wondering if these had anything to do with the incidents that kept occurring. It seemed unlikely my dad's parents had anything to do with all of this, but still, I wondered.

I opened the book, looking for any answers I may be able to find. *This is hopeless*, I thought, finding nothing. Surely if there was a hint somewhere, it had to be in here. I read over several more pages before closing the book, putting it down with a sigh.

I just couldn't understand why someone would assume I had any money. If I had, would I be living in this little duplex? Even I didn't know the answer to that, actually, since it was a great place to live. But, it wasn't a life of luxury by any means. And, I would certainly not be worried about the money the shop made each month; or worried if I'd even be able to keep the shop.

I was feeling hopeless when the phone rang. *LOGAN*.

Excitement bubbled up as I answered the phone. "What's up, Logan?"

I tried to keep my voice level, but I was sure a distinct crack was heard. Logan sure was having a big effect on me. One I both loved and hated.

"When you have a minute, could you come to my office? I think you should see something over here."

"Ok, sure. I will come over in about an hour. Can it wait that long?"

"That should be fine. Just needs to be as soon as you can." His voice held a hint of urgency. I wanted to press him for more information but realized it would be better to just get there.

I got dressed as quickly as I could and gathered my things. He'd sent me the address to his office, so I headed that way. A few minutes later, I knocked on Logan's office door.

I looked around Logan's office. Though I found it very sparse, it had clearly been recently ransacked. No artwork to be found, but Logan didn't really seem like an artwork kind of guy. The decor was simple, an oak desk, mismatched wood and cloth chairs, a credenza, and a fake Ficus in the corner.

Bridgette and I will have to give his Ficus a name, I thought to myself.

His window faced the alley and was extremely close to the brick wall of the next building. It wasn't very welcoming, which may not bother Logan, but likely would turn off some clients. Though, not as much as the state I currently found here would.

"What happened here?" I asked.

"I don't know. I came in this morning to find my office overturned, my files rummaged through, and a note left for me taped to my door handle."

Logan handed me an envelope. Inside, I found the note.

> *Give me all the information you can about the Winter's' estate. Gather it up and leave it in the mailbox at close of business today.*

"Why did they write Winters like this? With two apostrophes. It's like they don't even know if it is Winter or Winters. Which, I'm pretty sure would still only require it at the end either way." I set the note and envelope on his desk and bent down to pick up some strewn papers.

"Maybe they don't know. I do think I've narrowed it down. I believe it's Winter, singular. Whereas your grandparents are Winters, plural. The family that lost that huge sum that vanished, they had the last name of Winter, singular. So, I believe the person we are dealing with knows of the fortune belonging to the Winter family, but maybe it's been convoluted in research, and they think it's supposed to belong to the Winters family. Your family."

"Okay, but we aren't the only Winterses in the country. And I'm sure there are a lot of Winter families out there, too. Why would they think it's my family?" I placed the papers on a nearby table and plopped into one of the chairs.

"We need to give this place a make-over. Once all this is over, let me help with that. You need a more inviting space."

"You don't like my office?" Logan frowned. "What's wrong with it?"

"Uh, it's a little formal and cold. This is a warm, funky little town. You'll lose business with it being so, uh, brown. Every other business in town comes with a little flair in it, even the general store. That comes from Olivia, but still. This place needs a little livening up." I looked around the office again, nodding for emphasis.

"Okay, then, once this is all over, you can do what you will with the place. As long as it's still workable for my needs. Make it as, what was the word, funky, as you like. Also, make it easily moveable, because this is just temporary. Griffin and I are going in on the old mill with a friend." He smiled and it was a good thing I was sitting, because my knees would have given out.

"Good. I'll keep that all in mind," I said, regaining my composure. "Now, how do we get this person to leave me alone and realize they have the wrong person?"

Logan hesitated. "Until we know your mom's family history, I'm not entirely convinced they do, Kassidy. As for how we get them to leave you alone, I think that will take catching them. Or, really proving you are the wrong person."

"We can go talk to my mom soon. Neither of us know too much, but she'll know more than I do. I'm sorry, I wish I was more help there, but none of us were close to her side of the family. Once she married my dad, his family took her in as one of their own."

I shook my head, lowering it. I just didn't know what else to do. We'd found the family who was missing money, but it was just a case of mistaken identity.

"Sweets, look at me," he said.

My eyes snapped up. It was the first time he'd said that name out loud, and it was just as wonderful to hear as it was to read.

"We are going to figure this out. You're not alone in this, okay?" His blue eyes deepened with sincerity and his voice was steady, calming.

I nodded. His gentle compassion was what was sweet. I'm not even sure how I'd earned that term of endearment, but I never wanted to give it up.

"So, what are you going to do about their demands?" I asked.

"Nothing. I don't have anything for them, and even if I did, I don't give in to terrorist demands." He winked at me. Ugh.

"Logan? Could you not do that?" I asked, somewhat worried I'd damage some of the great time we had together.

"Do what?" he asked, worry and confusion suddenly lining his face. "Give them information?"

"No, winking. Could you not wink at me? I really hate it when people wink. Not sure why, just really don't like it."

He visibly relaxed and then laughed. "You got it, sweets. No more winking."

I smiled. This man. He was going to ruin me for everyone else, I could already tell. Maybe, if we could just get through this case, we could become something more.

"Well, I'm done for the day. Don't you have to be at the store at noon to work with Bridgette? Want to grab an early lunch before that?"

I looked around the office. Disaster still spread all around us. "Don't you want to clean this up?" I asked.

"I'll come back to it when you guys are working at the store. Then, I'll bring anything I need to work on over to the shop and keep you girls company while you work."

"You mean keep an eye on us while we work?" I teased.

"Eh, all the same, isn't it? You guys need a big, strong man over there to protect you if anything happens. Come on, a man's gotta eat."

He put his hand to the small of my back to lead me out, and warmth spread through my body. I willed him not to move his hand, and he didn't until I was safely at my car. I used the couple of minutes it took him to settle onto his bike to catch my breath.

It was also the first time I realized how he'd gotten around town. A motorcycle. Not a vehicle I'd ever pictured him driving, but it suited him somehow. Though he was so different from Sebastian in every way, seeing Logan on his bike seemed as natural to him as Sebastian's did. Logan pulled out of his spot, and I followed him to the pub.

Once there, we found Bridgette with Calliope and Trent in the corner booth. Our booth. One place in town that was still safe and welcoming. One place no thief could ever take away.

"Funny seeing you all together here," I said, the scene not something I'd have expected.

"We told you we'd try," Calliope said, though she looked tired.

Bridgette nodded in agreement and stuck a fry in her mouth as Logan greeted Trent, and they shared one of those bro chin dips.

"Logan, Trent. Trent, Logan," I said. "Trent and his family run the Equine Ranch that shares a property line with Calliope's farm. He's also her fella."

At that, Calliope giggled, and Trent groaned while Bridgette rolled her eyes. Logan laughed. A sound I was coming to love more and more every time I got to hear it.

"Nice to meet you, Logan. You watching out for our girl, here?" Trent asked, gesturing to me. A great reminder that this town was just one big family.

"Absolutely, not going to let anything happen to her while I'm around. I think we're on a good track to get this figured out soon." Logan sounded more confident than I felt, but I had no reason to doubt him.

"What are you guys doing here? You're both usually working right now," I asked, taking a fry off of Bridgette's plate.

"Doctor appointment," Calliope answered. Trent put a protective arm around his girl, but a tired, sad look crossed his eyes.

"Anything new?" Bridgette asked.

"No, not really. Except, they've diagnosed me with fibromyalgia and," she put air quotes around the and. "What that and is, we don't know yet. I have an MRI next week and more tests to go through. I have to go see a few more specialists to dig deeper."

She sighed. Bridgette and I did the same. We were almost carrying this right along with our friend, even if not as much. Trent absently rubbed Calliope's shoulder, and I knew he was probably hurting for her.

"Lucky for me, so far, my only answers mean there are no concrete answers. So, I just get to make new doctor friends, right?" Calliope's attempt at sarcasm did little to brighten spirits.

"I'm sorry, Callie. That sucks," I said. Everyone else nodded in agreement.

"It's okay, really. Some days are still so much better than they were months ago. I think the stress of everything just made it all worse. Anyway, the down time has given me some time to think, and I think your break ins are personal."

"What do you mean?" Logan asked before I could jump in. It seems we were both ready for any information that might lead us in a good direction.

"Well, when my notes came to me, the person obviously had intimate knowledge of me. I think the same is happening here. I think not only are they looking for something specific, but they know you intimately enough to know you are the one with whatever they are looking for. And just like he who shall not be named, they will escalate to get what they want."

"But, how could they know me that intimately? Everyone who knows me like that is here in this town." I said.

"Exactly. That's my point. I hate to say this, but I think it's someone we know from around town. It's someone who knows the town, knows your store, and likely knows ways to get you to wear down."

"You mean, like going after my friends?" I asked and glanced at Logan.

Whoever this was not only knew I was a target, but that Logan was helping me. They thought he had information. That's why they went after him at the office.

Calliope nodded. "Could be. If they think that friend has the information they need. I don't know. I was just thinking through the fact that they knew when to break in so you wouldn't be there. They were careful to take your keys and get into your home while you were distracted. That sounds like someone with knowledge about your background, routine. Like, they've been watching a while. That leads me to believe it's not a random outsider. It's someone here. How long they've been here, who knows, but that's beside the point."

"That all makes sense. I know I can't do a background check on the whole town, but maybe we can narrow it down to people of interest. I'll start helping you work on that," Logan said.

"When did the weird things start happening at the shop?" Bridgette asked her.

"Weird things?" Logan asked. I realized I hadn't told him of the strange occurrences that had been going on over winter break a few months back.

"Yeah, nothing big, just some odd occurrences at the bookstore. I guess could have been a precursor to this though. They started just around the time of the fires in December. There was so much going on then, and kids are bored at that time of year. So, I just brushed it off."

"Well, I know I haven't been much help so far, but hopefully that helps a bit. Maybe you guys can narrow it down and Logan can do some digging. Just wanted to give my two cents. But, now, I need some rest. This fatigue and pain are no joke, especially after a morning of being poked and prodded," Calliope said. She looked at Trent with starry eyes. "Take me home, my love."

"Yes ma'am," he said, and smiled.

They said their goodbyes and left us to think over what they'd said. It was close to noon now, so Logan and I got our food to go. We followed Bridgette out and across the square where Logan left us to get the store in order. We worked in silence as we waited for him to come back.

CHAPTER 11

BRIDGETTE AND I MADE quick work of getting things in order. Though we'd given ourselves three hours to put the shop in order, we realized it might take a little bit more time. We did our best with the time we had, and about half way through, true to his word, Logan was back with us.

"You here to be our bodyguard, tough guy?" Bridgette joked. I loved that they seemed to get along so easily. I had already decided I wanted Logan to be part of our group, and it would be that much easier if my friends liked him.

"Of course I am. Don't I look the role?" he asked, striking a pose with his biceps flexed. Bridgette and I both cracked up.

"Mhm, absolutely," Bridgette said, putting an old classic on the shelf in front of her.

"So, which of these books is your favorite? I'm guessing you both read a lot," Logan said, picking up one of the books on the cart we were using to organize.

"There are so many great books out there. It's so hard to choose. But one of my favorites is definitely Anthem, by Ayn Rand," I said. But, then five more books I loved sprang to mind. Still too many to choose. "Ooh, or The Outsiders by Hinton or Fahrenheit 451 by Bradbury. Man, there's just too many good ones to pick a favorite."

Logan laughed and put the book he was holding back on the cart. Since Bridgette didn't respond, he asked her directly. "What about you? Maybe some Austen? Pride and Prejudice? Emma? Are you a Darcy girl?"

"Ew, no, not even a little." She made a bit of a face before continuing, "I'm not much of a reader. I really only like two books. A Little Princess and Jane Eyre. I read them each a couple times a year.."

"What interesting favorite book choices. Why those?" He asked. I loved how interested he was in getting to know my friends, but I also knew she wouldn't get into that with him.

Darkness flashed in her features as she faced the shelf again. I knew she was feeling some hurt thinking of her answers to that question.

"I just like them, that's all," she said, focusing on the task.

I wanted to take the heat off of her, so I turned and instructed, "okay, take a seat out of the way to do your work, we're going to keep working on the store."

He tipped his head, questioning, and settled on one of the sofas. He didn't keep pressing her. I think he realized it wasn't the right time.

"Crazy to think this isn't random or that it's some outsider just getting things wrong. But that it's someone who has been watching you? That's so creepy." Bridgette shuddered after some silence.

She wasn't wrong. I hated knowing that by watching me, others were starting to be targeted too. I glanced at Logan and saw him studying the very note I was thinking of. His face was full of frustration. My stomach dropped.

Coming after my friends. This delusional person was moving beyond me and going after people I cared about. All for something I never had, something that didn't exist.

"Whatcha got there that's got you so miffed?" Bridgette said, calling attention to Logan and the harsh look he had staring at the note.

"Care if I share?" He asked. Like it was mine to say yes or no to. Or that I would deny my best friend information.

I shrugged. "Go for it. It was at your office."

"I was ransacked and left this note demanding all my information about Kassidy's case. They left it at my office." Logan's eyes flashed anger. This person was getting to him as much as they were me.

"So, it is personal. They are going after people close to the case now," Bridgette said with understanding. She went back to shelving books, focusing on the task. Almost as if to ward off the realization she'd just made.

"Yeah, so that means be careful. You and Griffin were both anxious to figure this all out. If this person thinks either of you have information, they could come after you, too. And, it might not just be a note. We don't know how far this person will escalate," Logan said, pinning Bridgette with a stern, warning look.

"But, they haven't been physical yet, right?" I asked. They haven't even shown themselves. To attack someone, you have to be right there, in their face.

"True, but if they get spooked or impatient, they may escalate. We can't take chances with anyone's safety."

Logan looked from Bridgette to me, concern all over his face. We both saw how serious he was, and we nodded. No sense in calling for more trouble when we were trying to get rid of trouble.

"Do we think," Bridgette started, and then stopped. It was quiet for a while.

"Think what?" I finally asked, unable to handle the silence.

"No, it's nothing."

"I know that voice, it's not nothing. It's something. It's something you don't want to say because it might upset me. I'm already freaked, so, out with it."

"Do we think it's weird that the person hasn't done much to you today? I mean, I know the note at Logans, but nothing toward you, specifically?"

"Could be they know they can't get in at the house or store or they've looked all they can at those places, so now, they are looking for other ways to get to her and to what they want," Logan said.

Honestly, I didn't care. I didn't want my friends to be harassed, but I also didn't want the person coming to my door anymore. I just wanted the nightmare to end.

Unfortunately, that wouldn't be happening any time soon if we didn't get more information. But since I didn't know how to get that, we turned our conversation to lighter topics as we arranged the store. We talked about going to the mainland for coffee supplies. Since Bridgette had to work the next morning, Logan agreed to take me, and Bridgette gave me cash that I could use to get started. I just loved my friends.

When three rolled around, Bridgette left to get ready for her shift at Brew & Bake while Logan and I locked up.

"I was thinking, if you're comfortable with it, you should stay with me until this is all over," Logan said as we went to the parking lot.

I stopped and looked at him. "I can't do that. I can't just leave my home because I'm scared. What kind of message does that send?"

"One that says you want to be safe?" he asked, as if it were just that simple.

"No. I can't. I can't leave Jessi there alone. Plus, I won't give this person the satisfaction of driving me from my home."

I knew he meant well, but just the thought of leaving my home and my neighbor vulnerable didn't sit well with me. As he'd discussed, this person could escalate, and then what?

"Okay, counter offer. I stay on your couch until we catch this guy."

I studied his face. He seemed serious, but I wasn't sure it was a good idea. Because, even if the person could escalate, it didn't mean they would. I didn't feel there was enough danger to uproot me and pull me from my home or to do the same to him.

"I don't know, Logan. That seems unnecessary, doesn't it? So far, everything has been done when no one is around. Like the person doesn't want to cause physical harm to people. Just find what they want and move on. Right?"

"Something just isn't sitting right for me, though. I don't like that you'll be alone. And, you don't have security in place yet."

"My dad's getting caught up on this job, he'll be out soon, I'm sure. I'll be okay. Jessi and I can keep ears out for one another."

"Okay, third proposition. I hang out with you until bed time, then make sure you lock up behind me. Then, I check everything out. Once I know you're safe, I will go home, but you keep me on speed dial. Final offer."

He was so serious, and I knew it was about keeping me safe. But there was something endearing about how he wanted to keep me safe by being in my company. I couldn't let it go.

"Why, Mr. Hart, if I didn't know any better, I'd swear you were just trying to spend time with me. If that's the case, all you have to do is ask." I gave a little laugh.

"Of course I want that, sweets. I'll take what time I can get." A smile crossed his lips and eyes but was quickly replaced with his serious look. "That's not what this is about though."

"I know. I'm just trying to lighten things up a bit. So many of my safe spaces have been tainted. And now they've come after you. I don't like thinking it will get worse."

Logan's arms engulfed me, pulling me to his lean chest. I let my head fall, feeling very at home in his arms. We stood there silently for a moment, neither wanting to break the moment.

"So, what will it be?" Logan finally spoke, not breaking the embrace.

I backed up to look him in the eye, my arms still partially around him. "Well, since you're so kindly giving me options, I guess option three. You just come hang out with me until I'm ready to hit the sack. Then you secure me in my home."

"Great. You know I'll be back first thing in the morning, right sweets? Long before we have to go to the mainland." He smiled.

"Yeah, I figured as much."

I was honestly surprised he wasn't planning on just staying in his car in my driveway all night. I didn't want to give him any ideas, so I kept my mouth shut.

"So, what should we do now?" I asked, not sure I really wanted to just go home yet.

"You could show me around town. Show me some of your favorite places." He grinned. This was a boyish, conspiratorial smile. Like he was in on a joke that I wasn't.

"We could do that. You've already been to the bookshop & the pub, which are two of my favorite places. But, there are a couple other places I can show you." Excitement flooded me at the thought of sharing some of the places that held special places in my heart.

"Lead the way," he gestured to my car.

"The last spot will bring us back here. Then we can get dinner at the pub and head home. It's not a huge island, so it's not like it'll take forever to show you these places." I smiled as he opened my door for me, and I slid behind the wheel. He got into the passenger side. "No fear in my driving abilities?"

"Should there be?" he asked, smile never leaving his face.

"Nah, I'm a great driver." I beamed. I steered us onto the main road that ran behind the inn and headed for the Scott's Christmas Tree Farm. Five minutes later, I pulled into a spot at the far end of the lot by the path to the tide pools.

They were an oddity for our little island, as we weren't technically at the ocean, yet here they were. Little pools teaming with life that adjusted based on the waters and seasons. A beautiful spot if ever there was one. The girls and I had come here often over the years, but I also came on my own a lot.

"A Christmas Tree Farm?" Logan asked as we got out.

"Actually, yes, this is one of my favorite places in fall and winter. Oh, and summer, when the gardens and conservatory are open. But, all of that is closed now for the off season as they do all the behind the scenes farming stuff. Summer here is great. And, the pumpkin patch and tree farm bring in so much business for the town. The Scotts have really made a name for themselves. But, that's not why we're here. Follow me."

I started down the path toward the tide pools, trusting Logan would follow. It was still colder than usual for that time of year, but much warmer than it had been in the last few days. I was thankful for a warm coat without much bulk. Even though I loved the beach in any weather, I knew we'd look pretty silly out on the beach in our coats.

I stopped where the trees opened up right to the beach and the trail ended in the coarse sand ahead. To the right were the tide pools and all the rest of the area was a small strip of sandy beach; a wonderful spot to spend a summer day with friends.

Logan came behind and broke the tree line. He stepped out onto the sand and looked around. "Wow, I didn't even know this place existed here." He said, voice full of awe.

Just how I felt every time I came here, especially now being able to share it with him.

"It's a local secret. It's a public beach, but most people assume it's part of the Scott's property, like the beaches by The Equine Ranch. But, it's not. We locals don't tell outsiders, though. It's nice to keep a local secret. I figure you're safe to tell. You can keep a secret, right?" I nudged him with my elbow and smirked.

"Yeah, I can keep a secret. As long as I get to come hang out with you here sometimes this summer." He nudged back. Our back and forth was so easy, but it gave me butterflies. I really should be focusing on all the danger happening. But, I found Logan to be a welcome distraction.

"Come over here, I want to show you the tide pools."

I led him over to the little pools. Persephone's favorite pastime here was to look for creatures. When we were younger, all the other girls were grossed out by it. I just wanted to look at all the fish. Knowing they were in their own little world we'd never fully understand. Just like me and my books.

After looking around for a bit, Logan said, "okay, where to next? I want to see all the great spots here on the island."

"Hm, okay, well, I showed you the Scotts' farms, which are great in different seasons. And, the tide pool beach.

Next, let's drive out to the other side of the island. The old Lighthouse is another of my favorite spots."

"Sounds good. Let's go."

We made it back to my car, and I was thankful for the opportunity to warm up as we drove to the other side of the island. It would likely be less than a ten minute drive, but still a chance to get out of the cold.

"So, the first day we met, you were a little pushy and gruff, yet here you are, Mr. Smiles. What was that about?" I asked him.

"Honestly?" He looked at me and I nodded. "I really wanted a chance to work on your case. I know Kinkaid and his team are doing fine, but I know they can't even consider the family with missing money as being tied to you. And, honestly, I'm having a hard time proving a link, either. They had a daughter who went missing around the time a big chunk of the money went missing, but they act as if she died. So, I don't know. I'm sorry. I've also been a bit pushy and cranky since the accident. I hate feeling like I'm less than I once was."

My heart ached for Logan. I could only imagine what that would be like. Having a career you love taken from you. And, it had to affect other areas of life, too. I couldn't imagine.

He turned the questions to me this time. "So, what was it like being an only child? Did you get lonely?"

"Not really. I had a great life growing up. And, the girls, especially Bridgette, became like my family. We played together often. It's just kind of the norm for my family. My great-grandma on my mom's side was an only child, my grandma was an only child. My mom had one sister, who she really doesn't get along with well. Then, me. My aunt never had kids. So, I had the girls, and Griffin. I was good."

"I can't imagine how quiet that house must have been. There are four of us; three brothers and a sister. We got loud. Our poor sister was probably losing her mind."

"So," I said as I parked in the post office parking lot; the closest one to the lighthouse. "Three boys and a girl. Where did she fit in the mix?"

"Next to last. My brother Landon, me, Lani, and Liam. We all treat her like the baby of the family, though. She and Liam are barely more than a year apart, so it got easy to do once he outgrew her when we were younger."

"Oh, yes, I'm sure she loves that," Logan laughed as I rolled my eyes as I led toward the lighthouse. I went on, "so, this is technically private property, but no one really cares. I don't really break a lot of rules, but everyone loves this lighthouse. I am hoping someone comes and buys it to turn it into a house or something so I can befriend them and hang out in the light house. Sometimes, I just like bringing a good book out here and sitting in the sunshine to enjoy the property."

"There's no fence, so how does everyone know where the property begins and when it becomes illegal to be here?" He wondered.

"We really honestly don't. But, no one does anything destructive to the lighthouse, so that's probably why we all get away with it."

I looked up at the magnificent structure. I've always loved lighthouses, there's something about the way they guide people back to shore and safety. A beacon of hope. This one hadn't been built for that, exactly, but it had that look, that beauty. I smiled.

"All your favorite places have been outdoors so far," Logan said, matter of factory.

"Well, other than The Bookshop and Brew & Bake, which are both inside. I love my friends' homes, but I can't just take you there and barge in. That leaves the outdoor spots. The Inn is a cute place, too, but we won't be getting a room, so no need to go there until they have an event."

"Makes sense. So, anywhere else? You said the last place would take us back over to near the parking lot."

"Yeah, it's almost silly to drive from here, but we will."

I drove us the two minutes back to the parking lot shared by Brew & Bake and the southeast side of the town square shops. Getting out, I led him to the grassy area of the town square, a bit away from the shops and the town hall. I picked my favorite spot and sat down, facing the clock tower on the Inn, watching the water beyond.

Logan sat down beside me and looked up. He took in the view all around and then glanced back to The Bookshop, which was just a shop away.

"Here? Really?"

"Mhm. Sitting here, looking at the Inn. Honestly, it's one of my favorite buildings on the island, like the lighthouse. I love the way the water looks behind and around the clock tower from this angle. It's so peaceful. I like to bring lunch out here on nice days. I've always thought this area was just so nice. And, it brings me joy. It calms me. It's like, the heart of the island and it centers me."

Logan nodded his understanding. I hadn't really shared this with anyone, not even the girls. Though, they knew this would be an easy place to find me if I wasn't home or at the shop. I found myself here more often than any of my other favorite outdoor spots. They just didn't know why.

Unfortunately for me, being out here meant Gideon and Huxley could keep eyes on me often. And, they did. I could never say why, but those two really gave me the creeps. Gideon really wanted total control of everything. He hated that so many of us were beyond his control.

Still, even with that, this spot was just a happy place for me. And, being able to share all these places with Logan made my heart burst. I wasn't sure what I was feeling for him, but I was hoping he felt the same.

Chapter 12

After a few minutes there just watching the water and the clock tower tick time away, I turned to Logan. "You ready?"

He nodded, and after he stood, he held his hand out to help me up. His hand felt warm and inviting, and I didn't let go after he helped me up. Neither did he. I marveled at the comfort of it all, as if we just naturally fit together.

Walking back toward the front of the shops, I noticed Gideon waiting outside the store. A chill ran down my spine as we got closer.

"Kassidy, just the person I was looking for," he leered. He never looked like he had a genuine thought in his head. Gideon was basically the equivalent of the town mayor.

Except, we didn't have a mayor. He was the only govern-ment official we had but having him as the head of the town council wasn't something anyone really liked.

Except for those in his organization. Something like a cult or fraternal organization. They were quite the sketchy group. One I knew no one my age or younger would be part of, which had been frustrating him a lot in recent years. He wanted complete control of the island and every-one in it. He made my skin crawl.

"What can I do for you, Mr. McKenna? We're closed right now." I asked, squeezing Logan's hand as if that would give me the strength to face whatever conversation Gideon was about to bring on.

"Yes, I'd heard about all that nastiness. That's why I stopped by. I wanted to remind you that if you ever need to get out of your lease, I'd be glad to help. Can't imagine you'd want to keep going after all of this. You know, I'll pay generously."

I gritted my teeth. The nerve he had, even to suggest buying my shop. Just because of some break ins. I knew he didn't want my shop so close to his and the pharmacy, but he also knew I'd never sell. And, the girls would never sell to him, no matter the amount of money he promised.

"First of all, no. I told you last year I would never be selling to you. So did Nehemiah and Ruth, and the girls would agree. We aren't selling to you. Second, I'm not letting a few break ins destroy me. Got that?"

"It seems you're not ready. I see that. But, don't make a foolish mistake. I know this is costing you greatly, and I know you've already been struggling to stay afloat. You will need my deal in time. I'll be here when you do."

He gave a decisive nod of his head and turned to go back to the general store. I couldn't even speak. I felt the heat rise in me as my anger grew.

"Wow, what a jerk," Logan muttered next to me, giving my hand a reassuring squeeze.

"Honestly, he's the worst. He's really upset he can't get my shop. He already owns the pharmacy and the general store. I think he just wants to expand. We all know he wants to take over this town, have this whole island be for his weird little cult group. Forcing out anyone else. I think he's realizing he's losing power, though."

"Why is he losing power?" Logan asked, guiding me toward the pub.

"Most of the older generation that has been with him have gotten over his antics. Like Sebastian's parents. I know they left the organization, along with some others. Then, the next two generations, ours and those after us, just have no desire to bend to his will. We all see right through his crap and need for control. With people moving in and out of town, too, he just loses it more and more."

"People who lose power like that, whether they really had it before or not, tend to get unstable. Do you think that could be him? Could he be behind everything, just trying to get you to sell?"

"I guess, he could, but why now? Especially since he hasn't brought up the sale in six or more months. I feel like he's just sleazy, just taking advantage of the situation. Honestly, he thrives off of fear, but I don't think he's the one doing this."

Logan nodded and dropped my hand to open the door. We ordered some food to go and waited by the bar.

"Hey guys," Persephone greeted, coming in quickly, Calliope close behind. Worry lined both their faces. "Have you seen my notebooks for class? I had them when I was studying at The Bookshop before the big break in. But, I thought I took them home later. I can't find them."

I shook my head as Sebastian appeared in the doorway of the game room. A storm gathered behind his eyes as he watched Persephone. Something protective brewed in his gaze.

"Sorry. They definitely weren't at the shop," I said. I looked from her to Logan to Calliope. Persephone looked back at her sister. "You're sure you never saw them at the house?"

Calliope shook her head, and Persephone's face fell. She went from worried to dejected, and it looked like tears weren't too far away. "It's okay, I'll go check with Bridgette."

Persephone hurried off to find Bridgette, who was cleaning up tables in the game room. Sebastian followed her in there, and I looked back at my friend.

"Is everything okay there?" I asked Calliope.

"She's been so stressed since everything happened. Keeps forgetting things, losing things. I don't know. Something feels off. I feel like something is really wrong, beyond what happened in December, but she's just not ready to talk. The last few months have been the hardest we've ever been through, you know. It seems to really be getting to her." Concern dripped from my friend's voice as she watched her sister talk to Bridgette.

My heart ached for both of them. I knew it had been such a hard time over the last few months. I hated that Calliope sometimes felt she brought all the trouble to town. Especially since it seemed now the trouble was following me.

"So, what about you? How can I help?" She looked from me to Logan.

"Your tip earlier was helpful. Knowing we're looking for someone who knows me is helpful. I wish the police had more," I said.

"I wish I had more," Logan ground out through gritted teeth. A look like the one I'd seen when Sebastian looked at Persephone passed his eyes. Something in the water recently made the Miller's Pointe guys very protective of their women. *Their women. His woman.* I smiled at the thought.

"Well, if I can do anything else, let me know. You know, I'm apparently always ready to run into a burning building," Calliope laughed.

"You know I'm not going to be asking you to do that. But, if you see or hear anything around town, let me know. Other than that, just keep yourself well, okay?"

"You got it," she said, as Persephone came back over.

"Not here, either. Not at Sebastian's house. I don't know where they could be or what I'm going to do. Let's go home." Persephone tugged on Calliope's sleeve, and they were out the door.

Our food came just then, and we took it back to my house. We opted for a movie with dinner, and I really enjoyed having a night of normalcy. Or, I tried to enjoy a night of normalcy.

I couldn't get the conversation with Gideon out of my head, though. And, the questions Logan had asked. And,

Calliope's tip that this was all personal. Maybe it really could be as simple as Gideon wanting to buy my shop, but something didn't feel right about that.

Once the movie was over, we found ourselves playing games. True to his word, Logan didn't leave until I was beyond tired and ready for bed. Then, true to his word again, he was back at sunup the next day. Long before I'd come close to being ready to go to the mainland for supplies.

Chapter 13

As Logan waited for me to get ready, my phone rang. My mom's name flashed on the screen. I really didn't want to talk to her or my dad about what had been going on, but I couldn't just ignore her call.

"Hello?" I answered, trying to decide between two pairs of leggings.

"Kassidy, sweetheart, I'm sorry to call so early. Did I wake you?" She sounded worried, more freaked out than usual. Like something was wrong, but she was trying to hide it.

"No, I was awake. What's wrong, mom?" I chose one of the pairs without thinking just to get them on.

"Well, your dad didn't want me to call, but I thought you should know. We had a break in at the house this morning. We think the guy didn't know we had an alarm, and didn't expect the police to live so close, so he ran off before any damage could really be done. I mean except the window he broke. But, we're all safe. Just, shaken, as you can imagine."

My mom was rambling. She did that when she was anxious, and it was a trait I'd inherited from her. My stomach knotted. Obviously this had to be related to what was going on here, which automatically ruled out Gideon. He'd have no reason to go after my parents. But, manipulate the situation, that he'd do.

So, who else could be doing this? What was going on? Was Logan right all along, and there was family money somewhere related to my mom's family?

My mind was reeling, I barely registered my mom breaking my thoughts. "Kassidy? Are you there?" She asked.

"Yeah, mom, sorry. I'm here. I'm so sorry. I'm on my way, okay? I'll be there soon."

"You really don't need to come. I just wanted you to know. Everything here is fine, honest."

"I already have plans to go to the mainland. I'll go earlier than planned and stop by your house.

Logan will be with me. He's been helping me with some stuff at the shop and with the break ins. We'll be there soon."

"Oh, sweet girl, you have too much to worry about. This is probably nothing. I just thought you should know. But, if you do come, we'll take you guys to brunch or lunch. Okay?"

"Sounds good, mom. We'll be there, soon."

We said our goodbyes, and I didn't even think too much about the rest of my outfit as I hurried to get ready. Logan was waiting on my couch.

"Ready already?" he asked, smiling at me. Then, his mood suddenly shifted. "What's wrong?" Clearly my concern was written all over my face, and I was hurried. I just wanted to get to my parents' house as quickly as I could.

"My parents' house was broken into this morning. The person couldn't do much because of the alarm and police response. But, I think it's the same person. We need to get to the ferry. It leaves in fifteen minutes, or we have to wait another two hours."

He was up and out the door faster than me, opening the driver side door for me. I slid in, and he was in the passenger seat in a flash.

We made it to the ferry in time, but I couldn't stop the knot from growing in my stomach. Adding strands with each negative thought I had.

Thoughts about the break ins, my parents' lives being disrupted. Thoughts about Logan having more on his plate because of me. Thoughts of Gideon trying to use this all to his advantage.

I knew it wouldn't unravel until we got all our answers, but I didn't know how long someone could live with a knot in their bellies.

I took a deep breath once we were in my parents' driveway. I saw my dad walking around, checking the perimeter. Mom must have been inside somewhere. We approached my dad who drew me into a big, protective hug.

"Kassidy, you didn't have to come out here," he whispered before kissing my head.

"I know, but Logan and I were already going to be out this way. Oh, dad, this is Logan. You haven't had a chance to meet yet. He's investigating the break ins as a private investigator."

My dad gave Logan a firm handshake and looked him over. "Nice to meet you, son. Any payment you need once this case is solved, you let me know. Got that?"

"Nice to meet you, too, sir. But, as for money, I have smaller cases paying me. I'm not charging Kassidy for this one."

I looked at him in shock. We hadn't discussed money yet. I honestly hadn't thought about it at all, or that this is how he made his living.

Now, I felt weird that he was doing this without payment.

"Well, then, you have my thanks," my dad said. I smiled up at my dad, his arm still around me.

"I'm going to go find mom," I said, pulling away.

"Logan, son, why don't you help me out here for a bit. I'm just trying to see if there was only one entry point or see if there is anything else out of place. I could use a good pair of eyes."

"He did pass the detective exam, so he'll probably come in handy with the details," I said, knowing my dad didn't know about Logan's accident or eye problems. I beamed proudly at the man who'd gone out of his way to help me.

"Great," my dad clasped Logan's shoulder. "Let's get to work."

Logan followed my dad, and they started looking at the perimeter of the house. Something about my dad and Logan together made my heart happy. I watched just a bit longer before I went and found my mom in the kitchen.

"Hey mom, can I ask you some questions about Great Grandma?" I asked her, watching Logan as he assessed the house. I knew he was asking my dad all about the security system and cameras and if they'd caught anything.

Lucky for my parents they lived so close to the police station. That's probably why the intruder hadn't gotten further than the front room, but Logan didn't want to take any chances. My dad didn't say it, but I could see he found that endearing about Logan.

"Sure, but I don't know how much I'll be able to tell you. Ask away, baby."

"Do you know what her last name was? Or where she came from?"

"You know, I really don't. All I knew was she wasn't in contact with her family anymore and something bad happened that caused it. I knew she met your great grandpa, they fell in love, and your grandma was born. But, you know she and my mother weren't ever close. And, unfortunately, neither were my mom or Susan and me."

I nodded. I knew that side of the family wasn't super close. I'd seen my grandma several times through the years, but I think she was closer to me than to my mom. My aunt Susan was very distant. She never had kids, so I had no cousins on that side. It all seemed so sad and lonely to me.

"Do you know what her maiden name was? Great Grandma's I mean? And, did they have a lot of money?"

Mom thought about this, her face contorted as if she was trying to gather information from the air. "I don't think there was a lot of excess money. They lived modestly, but comfortably. My mom never wanted for anything. She was able to get her education. So, it was enough to live, but not wealth that I know of. None of us ever saw it, anyway. As for her maiden name, I honestly don't know. Wingate. Winchester. Something like that?"

"Something that may have sounded like Winter or Winters?" I asked. That seemed a bit coincidental.

"Something like that, I think. But I really don't know. I'm sorry Grandma isn't around to answer that for you. You know she'd tell you anything she knew."

"Did Great Grandma leave any sizable money to Grandma or you and Susan when she passed?"

"No, she and Great Grandpa had a little money that they left to Grandma, and she got more from the sale of the house. But, that wasn't a lot and Susan and I never got any of it. Most of the art was left to her local libraries and historical society and places like that. Susan and I each got a piece. Mine is the one hanging in your duplex. Then, we got a couple of journals of your great grandma's and some furniture. But that was about it. Why are you asking all this?"

"Just trying to solve the mystery of what this person is after. We know it can't be from dad's side, so I'm just curious, I guess. Logan has this idea in his head, so we wanted to ask and see if there was a connection. At this point, I just don't know. And, I'm so, so sorry I brought this problem to your door."

I broke down. Everything felt hopeless, like we were looking in circles. We were dogs chasing their tales, and there was no end in sight. Now, the person had come after my parents. I couldn't handle it.

My mom came and wrapped her arms around me. "Baby girl, listen to me. This person, if it is the same person, is after something that doesn't exist. Your dad and I are more worried about you and your safety than anything we have in this house. It makes me feel so much better knowing you have Logan and all your friends looking out for you. We'll be fine. I promise."

Her words brought so much comfort, just like a mother's words should. It made me sad she didn't have that with her own mom or sister, and then I was crying for a whole different reason. I let my mom hold me until I heard Logan clear his throat from the doorway.

"Logan, come in, sit down." My mom released me and gestured to the couch next to me on the other side.

He sat down and didn't hesitate to put a protective arm around my shoulder, while my mom moved to the love seat. My dad joined her there, putting his hand in hers. One day, I really wanted to have what they had.

"Well, everything is looking fine here. Just that broken window. If the person was able to disarm your security system, they either didn't know we had one or just took their chances. I've got a friend coming in to help me replace the window in a couple hours, and I'm going to get a few more cameras. But, other than that, we're all set, Kassy-bean. Your mom and I will be fine, but I wonder if maybe you should come stay here until they figure this all out."

"I can't do that. I have the shop. I'd hate to leave Jessi all alone. If something happened, I'd never forgive myself." I sighed. This really felt like a losing game.

"Why don't you take your great-grandma's journals. Maybe you'd learn her maiden name or something more about why she left or what happened," mom suggested. She went to get them.

Logan finally spoke, looking directly at my dad, "I'll make sure we keep an eye on her, sir. The whole town is on alert, it seems. I've got friends and contacts helping me figure out who is doing this and why. We'll catch them.

And, until we do, I'll do my absolute best to keep Kassidy safe."

"I know you will, Logan. We can't tell you how much we appreciate that. You be careful with her, too, you hear me?" My dad said, an unspoken understanding passing between them. One I wasn't emotionally ready to unpack in that moment.

Mom came back in and handed me three leather bound journals. They were beautiful. If you didn't know they were journals, they would look like they fit in the rare first edition classic section of my shop. I held on to them like they were my only lifeline, and I was drowning.

"Well, now that we've got all the ugliness out of the way, how bout we take you two out for a good meal. Logan, you look like a boy who knows how to eat."

Logan laughed, "yes, ma'am. I have two brothers, I learned to grab what I wanted quickly before there was nothing left. Too bad for our baby sister."

We all laughed, and I loved how easily Logan fit with my parents. My parents were all I had left, since I was an only child. I hated to think like that, but as they aged, I couldn't help it from time to time. They were still young, barely out of their 50s, but it was still something that came to mind every now and then. Seeing a man I was falling for fit so well with them made my heart soar.

Even if I'd barely admitted it to myself until now, I couldn't deny it anymore as I watched him that morning with my family and hearing him share about his family. His childhood sounded much louder than mine, except for when all the girls were on the island to visit. They were the closest I had to sisters, and I loved them. Still, hearing about all the antics with Logan's siblings reminded me it wasn't the same.

After brunch, we made sure my parents were back and settled, and said goodbye just as my dad's friend came to fix the window with him. Logan offered to stay and help, but they shooed him away. My mom sent him home with some of her homemade salsa and sweet tea, and he just ate up all the attention.

"You okay?" he asked on the way home.

"I'm exhausted, honestly. I think I felt every possible human emotion today, and we still aren't any closer to solving this puzzle. I hate that it has now affected you and my parents. What if my mom had been home? What if the police hadn't gotten there? So many what ifs."

"Kassidy, sweets, listen to me. You can't play the what if game," he said, his voice soft, but firm. "It will destroy you, and we all need to be focused until this is all over."

"You're absolutely right. No more what ifs, just facts. Speaking of facts, what did you and my dad talk about this afternoon? He and my mom both seem to like you. I think they plan to adopt you."

"Oh, they won't be adopting me, but it's nice to know you think they'd let me be part of the family." I turned and saw his face light up with a smile. "We talked about his security system. Damage that was done. Where we think the intruder went. You."

My heart skipped a beat when he said that last word. "Me?"

"Yeah, you. He's so proud of you, you know that? Your parents love you a lot. He made me promise to take care of you. He said you'd never agree to go stay with them. I let him know I'd be there to keep you safe."

"Really? How do you plan to do that?" I asked.

"I have my ways. Mostly, I don't plan to ever leave you alone if I can help it. I'll make sure Griffin or Bridgette or Trent or Callie can come hang out with you. I plan to work from the store once you get it open again. And, any time I can be with you, I will be with you."

I wasn't expecting him to plan to stick so closely to me. It made me warm inside, and my stomach twisted in the best way. I tried to tell myself it was just him taking his job seriously, but something told me it was more than that. Logan wanted to protect me because I was special to him. At least, that's what I was starting to let myself believe.

CHAPTER 14

ONCE BACK ON THE island, I convinced Logan to take me to check in at the store before going home. We were almost opened back up, but since I needed to go see my parents, I had Persephone watch and organize the store. The minute she looked at me, I knew something was wrong. Logan did, too.

"What's wrong?" he asked, concern filling his voice and the space around us.

"Some guy came in earlier and asked for you. I told him you were out on emergency. He was a bit gruff. Anyway, when I told him you were out, he scribbled a note for you. He folded it up and handed it to me, but I read it. I think he might be the one you're looking for. But, I didn't know that until he was long gone. I'm sorry. I let you down."

Persephone looked completely broken. More than she had the last few months. More than she had even yesterday. My heart ached for my young friend. This was just one more thing to strip her of her vibrancy, a quality of hers we were all beginning to miss.

I wrapped my arms around her. "It's okay, Perse. We'll see if we can get his face off the store footage. Can I see the note?"

She handed me the folded paper.

> ***Give me the money I'm owed, otherwise I'll have to start hurting people.***

Strange, considering the only people I owed money to were Persephone, Calliope, and Shiloh; and I knew none of them would be doing this.

I handed the note to Logan. He read it and then crumpled it in his hand. Anger flashed in his eyes, and he moved closer to Persephone and me.

"This guy is delusional. I don't owe anyone money. At least not in any way to call for this."

"What do you mean by that? Who do you owe money to?" Logan asked, trying to keep a reign on his anger. His eyes were burning. If he wasn't on our side, I'd be terrified.

"Thanks to this debacle, I'm a week behind on my payment to the girls. That's it."

"I swear, this isn't us, Kass. I swear," Persephone said, fear in her eyes. Fear and exhaustion.

"We know this isn't you guys, Persephone," Logan reassured, somehow keeping his voice calm. "We'll take a picture of this and then get it to Kinkaid. Let's get a look at that camera footage."

Luckily, we had just got the security system back up, courtesy of my dad's team. I pulled up the store's feed from that day and rewound it until we found the guy in question. Unfortunately for us, his face was never visible on camera. Blocked by a hat and skillful avoidance, we never had a clear shot.

"It's okay, I had a feeling," Persephone said. She stepped over to the counter and pulled out her sketchbook. Persephone's art skills rivaled anyone I'd ever known. "I made a few sketches of him. Front view. Profile view."

"You should be a forensic sketch artist," Logan said, admiring the drawings.

If this weren't a man terrorizing me and destroying my life, it would be a masterpiece. She captured his essence, and it was right there on the page. He was gruff. He looked angry, hard. No doubt after something.

Persephone shrugged. "Not my thing, but in this case, I thought it might be important. I wrote down the other things I would remember, too. Hair

and eye color, height. What he was wearing. Whatever might be helpful."

"Thank you so much. I feel like this is the first positive thing to happen in this case." I gave her another hug.

"I'll get pictures of the note and these sketches, then I'll get it all to Kinkaid. He'll want to use these to find this guy. I'll also run them with my contacts. We'll get this figured out. Kassidy, do you recognize this guy?" Logan asked.

I looked at the papers again and shook my head. I'd never seen this guy a day in my life. But I guess if someone isn't thinking straight, that wouldn't matter.

Logan nodded, then took the papers outside with his phone to call Kinkaid. I took the first full breath I'd taken in several days. One step closer to getting this nightmare to end.

Before long, Kinkaid was in The Bookshop, images in hand, asking me and Persephone questions. No, we didn't know who he was. No, I didn't owe anyone other than the girls. No, we didn't know what money the guy was talking about.

Finally, he had all he needed, after asking the same questions over and over in new ways. I assume trying to see if our answers changed. Of course, they didn't, because we weren't lying. I knew he was just being thorough, but I couldn't help feeling more like the suspect than the victim.

I hated how this was dragging on with no answers. Kinkaid and Logan both promised answers would be coming soon. Both were pretty sure they had resources to identify the guy and put an end to everything.

"Let me give you both a ride home," Logan offered, knowing Persephone had been dropped off.

"That's okay. I'm going to the pub to meet Olivia and the guys. I'll be fine," Persephone said, gathering her things.

"Thanks again for those drawings, Perse. I can't even tell you how amazing that help is, especially without the cameras."

"I'm just glad I could help. Who knew art could be so tactical?" She grinned before she left.

Logan and I followed her out before going to my house. I let him in, knowing I wouldn't be able to convince him to leave this time. Not with the break in at my parents and threat at the shop. I'd be surprised if he left my side any time before this guy was behind bars.

Confirming my suspicion, he called Griffin to bring him some clothes, letting him know that he'd be on my couch for the foreseeable future. I felt like arguing, but it wouldn't do any good. After all, I wasn't sure if I could handle myself if this guy actually did come after me.

As Logan busied himself on the phone, I pulled out one of the journals my mom gave me.

Not much was in it. All just about how she was in love with my great grandpa, and they were expecting. Nothing about family secrets or money. Just pregnancy, and life as a new mom. I did notice my great grandma seemed to be going through some postpartum depression, not that they had that name for it back then, but maybe that's why she was never as close to my grandma. I wasn't sure.

But, before I could look into either of the other two journals, my eyes grew heavy, and I was ready for bed. I got some bedding and pillows for Logan to set up on the couch and went to bed. I fell asleep with questions about the past week swirling in my head, no answers anywhere to be found. The last thing I remember before sleep overtaking me was the image of Persephone's drawing. The man who was destroying my life.

Chapter 15

A few days passed with no incident. I was able to open the shop and loved seeing everyone back out to support the re-opening.

One thing about this town was that they were always there to support someone in times of need. My friends were all there to check in on me. Griffin came in with all kinds of questions, asked permission to run a story with the images of the guy. Shiloh came from the mainland to check in, even though she still had a few weeks left at her job. Calliope kept eyes and ears open, ready for battle, no matter how much I told her to stand down. Bridgette was at my side whenever she could be, and Logan literally never left my side.

"Taking no chances. Promised your dad," he'd said. And that was that. My own personal bodyguard was with me all the time.

I didn't mind much, though, because even though it had been a few days of no incident, I couldn't let myself breathe. I wasn't naive enough to believe that it was over. The guy was just lying low, trying to figure everything out.

It had been so busy our first few days open that I mostly worked and slept. I tried to sleep in as much as I could, but it really wasn't much. My body and mind were just on too high alert for that.

After that few days of calm, the storm returned with a vengeance. My phone rang at six a.m. *BRIDGETTE.*

"This better be good," I said, not even letting my eyes open again.

"Kassidy, I. He." Bridgette was stammering, and her usual humorous tone was replaced with terror, her voice thick with tears.

My eyes shot open. "He, who?"

"The guy from the pictures. He's dead. Someone shot him. Kinkaid is on his way. But, you need to get Logan and get over here."

"What? Dead? Shot? What?" I stammered, trying to get myself out of bed. My sheets seemed to have a death grip on me, and I tripped out of bed instead.

Logan rushed in, finding me on the floor, phone having been flung by the door. He picked it up and gave it to me before helping me unravel myself.

"Kassidy? You there? Are you coming? I'm over by the Lighthouse. I was on my way to the pub when I saw him. You have to come here. Please."

I'd never heard Bridgette so freaked out. Anyone would be by seeing a dead body. But, to see the main suspect who had been harassing your friend? That was enough to get to anyone.

"I'm on my way with Logan. Okay, it's going to be okay. We're getting ready now to go." I disconnected the call and looked to Logan.

He looked confused but ready.

"That was Bridgette. She found our suspect. He's been shot. She's freaking out."

He nodded, leaving me to get dressed. I threw on clothes and found him waiting by the door. Just like a boy scout, always ready.

We got to the scene just as Kinkaid pulled up. He was barking an order at someone to get Persephone out to the scene to make an ID, which I thought was a little excessive with the pictures we had.

I gave Bridgette a hug and we stood off to the side, Logan close by. We watched as Kinkaid assessed the scene.

"Why do I keep finding you at my crime scenes, Bridgette?" He glared at her, practically ignoring me.

"Your crime scene? I don't see your name on it, and last I checked, no detective badge, either, sunshine." She gave him a look I knew was her angry-flirty look. She didn't use it often, but if she did, it was a guy she couldn't decide if she wanted to kiss or kill.

He flashed a badge and said, "actually, I just got promoted during the few days you all managed to stay out of trouble. Don't touch anything around here, and if you have a statement, we'll need it."

Kinkaid still hadn't looked my way. Something was passing between him and Bridgette, and it wasn't lost on me. "You two know each other, I take it," I said.

They both looked at me, clearly having forgotten anyone else was around. As much as I wanted to know what was going on with my best friend and this newly promoted detective, I really wanted to know what was going on with the man under the tarp.

"Oh, we go way back," Bridgette spat out, sarcasm dripping from her words. "And I do have a statement. I'm the one who found him here."

"Okay, this officer over here will get your statement. Ms. Winters, a word please." Kinkaid waved another officer over and sent him with Bridgette before turning his attention to me.

"Congrats on your promotion, Kinkaid," I said before he could get any questions out.

"Thanks. Look, are you sure you don't know this guy?" He asked.

"No, I honestly have never seen him before. Just the pictures Persephone drew."

Kinkaid nodded. "He had your business card on him when he was shot. As a a matter of fact, he was holding it when he died. We don't have a phone for him anywhere. No ID or wallet or anything."

Logan placed a protective arm around my waist, and I pulled closer to him. I shook my head. "I honestly don't know him."

Kinkaid nodded and jotted down notes. He asked a few more questions before Persephone arrived and he took her over for the ID. She gave a nod of her head and turned away. I looked off to the side to see Trent, who pulled Persephone into his arms. The older brother she'd never had, but who would likely actually be her brother soon enough.

I saw Bridgette talking to Kinkaid for a moment before she walked over to me and Logan. She was practically fuming. "Ugh, the nerve of that guy."

"Who is he to you?" Logan asked.

"I've only had a few run ins with him. But he's so arrogant. He drives me crazy. Can't wait for this case to be wrapped up."

"Seems like you might protest too much," Logan joked. He really was perceptive.

A look flashed on Bridgette's face. One I'd only seen a handful of times. The last one being when she realized Trent would only ever be her friend. It was a look that screamed desire and defeat in the same moment. Usually, she was able to keep men at arm's length. But I knew that look for her. That look meant trouble.

"Let's get out of here. I don't want to be around this stuff anymore. I'm already late for the pub. Let's go."

I took one last look at the scene by the lighthouse. Another safe place of mine ruined. A life lost, related to my shop and the break ins. Definitely an escalation. And, somehow, it felt like it was all my fault.

CHAPTER 16

THAT AFTERNOON, I WAS sitting across the square staring at the hotel clock tower. Logan had to take care of some things, so I managed to shake him for a while. I promised not to go anywhere, that I'd stay in my shop; but I found myself here. One last safe spot left on the island. For now. Something about the Inn always calmed me; it was a gorgeous building. So much was going on around me recently, I felt like it could all collapse at any moment.

"People have been worried about you," Logan's words cut through my thoughts.

"I figured," I said, not trusting myself to look away from the tower.

"I know this is hard for you, but your friends are worried you turned your phone off, won't talk to them. But, they wouldn't come looking for you because they wanted to respect your right to privacy."

"So, you found me, then?" I asked. My gut clenched & tears threatened to break free from my eyes. I knew he'd come looking for me. Still, my mind and body reacted now that he was actually here.

"I would rather just make sure you're okay. If you want to be alone, I'll be alone with you. Told you, until we figure this out, I'm not going anywhere. Promised your dad, too, so you're stuck with me."

I felt him sit right next to me. His presence was strong, but comforting. I stayed quiet, enjoying the view of the clock tower and the water beyond. Finally, I broke the silence, still not daring to look at him.

"Okay, so, why is it so important to you to make sure I'm okay? To stay by my side, even when it's so obvious I want to be alone." *Or that anyone close to me is in danger*, I thought.

Silence. Maybe it was the wrong thing to ask; but suddenly, I was desperate to know. Like his answer would mean everything.

"Kassidy, look at me," he said, his voice steady, sure. I wasn't sure I could do that. "I can't answer that question without looking you in the eyes, sweets."

His tone softened but stayed just as sure. I looked him in the eye.

"When this is all over - and it will be over soon - I want you to know there's more to me than just work and getting answers. I work just as hard on all my cases, but this isn't just about a case. You are something special. And, when it's all over, I plan to make it about more than just coming together over a bad circumstance. So, I'm taking every opportunity to show that I'm with you."

His face was soft, but certain. His eyes bore into mine, willing me to believe everything he said. And, I really had no reason not to, except that I hadn't even wanted to consider my own feelings beyond this case, even if my mind forced me to consider it anyway.

I was considering them now, and it overwhelmed me. I tore my gaze from his and put it back on the scene that centered me. Not wanting to think about anything beyond the scene in front of me. Not the man we saw murdered this morning. Not the break ins. Not the guy next to me who was trying to protect me, even if it meant not giving me any time alone.

We sat in silence for several more minutes before I finally said the only word that had been playing in my head for so long. "Why?" It barely came out a whisper.

"Why, what, Kassidy?"

That did it, the floodgates of questions opened, starting with the most recent.

"Why me? Why do you think you want that with me with so much drama around me? And, why me? Why would this person assume that my family had money? Or, if they did, why would I know about it? Why destroy the only suspect we had? Why not keep the heat off of them? And, why me?"

"Sweets, I can't answer most of those questions. I can only answer the one about me. Why you? Because you're caring and determined and even in all of this, oh so trusting. And you're the most beautiful woman I've ever known. Inside and out."

I looked at him, incredulously. He let out a laugh. "What?"

"You've met my friends, right?" I couldn't keep it from coming out of my mouth.

His brows furrowed in confusion. "Yeah, I've met them. And?"

"Callie's got the curves. Persephone's practically a model. Bridgette is an exotic, gorgeous queen. And, you've seen

Shiloh and Olivia, too, right? Then, there's me" I gestured down over my body and my face.

I knew I wasn't ugly by any stretch of the imagination, but I also knew I wasn't even close to being in the running for most beautiful woman in the world. I was just, normal.

His face grew even more confused, taking me in. I grew more and more uncomfortable under his gaze, so I looked away again.

"Kassidy, sweets, look at me when I say this." He grabbed my hand and waited for me to look at him. I finally brought my eyes to his face. "I've met all of those women. And, to me, they have nothing on you. Are they each beautiful in their own way? Sure, but you're it for me. Got it?"

He was so sure of himself, so sure of me, all I could do was nod. I wish I had the same confidence.

He started laughing a big laugh. "Do you women always do that?"

"Do what?" I asked, my eyes snapping back to his face, completely confused.

"Compare yourselves to each other and ignore your own beauty?"

"I guess it depends," I shrugged. "I don't know if we all do it, but yeah, a lot of us do."

He just shook his head. We sat in silence for a bit longer before we decided to go get dinner. Somehow, I wasn't upset my alone time was ruined for the afternoon. I found with everything going on that I preferred being alone with him to being alone-alone.

I wasn't sure what that meant for us when this was all over, but I had a feeling, I'd be okay with the arrangement he'd mentioned earlier in the afternoon. We just had to get through the crazy first.

We took dinner back to my place and found Jessi waiting on the porch.

"Oh, my goodness, Kassidy are you okay?" She rushed to hug me.

"Yeah, it's been a long few days, but I'm doing okay." I hugged her back, but it felt so awkward since she and I had never been that close before.

"I'm so glad. After your parents' break in and now this guy who was the suspect being killed and all. I saw it on the news. Officer Kinkaid said they were wanting any information. How scary."

Jessi looked so panicked, and I hated that I'd brought all this stress to Miller's Pointe, even if it wasn't actually my fault. I hated seeing Logan forced to spend all his time with me rather than other cases. I hated seeing worry lining Bridgette and Calliope's faces all the time.

"I really am okay. I'm sorry you are being so affected by this madness. If you don't want to keep up with your lease, I'm sure my parents will understand," I said, realizing she probably wasn't happy with her living arrangement now.

She waved me off. "No, no. It's not your fault. I'm fine right here. If you need anything, I'm right next door."

She gave me one last look and then gave a strange look to Logan. One I couldn't quite place. He caught the change too, as she walked back into her own unit.

"I don't think your neighbor likes me much," he said as we took our food inside.

"I don't know. She's kind of a loner, keeps to herself. Maybe something else is going on that you remind her of."

I set about getting our food ready and we settled on the couch. We ate in comfortable silence, neither of us hurried to do anything else. Just like the afternoon at the town square, it was a breath of fresh air during the crazy events of recent days.

"That was great. Bud and Mabel know what they're doing over there at the pub," Logan said as he finished off his piece of pie.

His appetite stayed in place, where mine had completely disappeared. I ate only because everyone was making me at this point. I didn't think I'd enjoy a meal again until all of this was behind us.

Logan got up and started walking around the living room, searching for something. Like the first time he'd been looking for bugs.

"What are you doing?" I asked, watching him work.

"Something feels off. I just want to make sure nothing has happened. No listening devices or anything." He kept going from the living room to the kitchen.

I got up to follow. "Okay, but there weren't any last time. Now, we have new locks and the security alarm my dad put in. I don't think you're going to find anything."

"Then humor me, okay?"

I nodded and followed him around the kitchen. When he found nothing, he gestured down the hall to the bedrooms. I nodded and he went back to business. Nothing in the office or bathroom - thank God about that one. How creepy that would be.

"I told you," I said as he started the bedroom, but stopped just as quickly as he picked something from the nightstand.

He lifted a finger to his lips to silence me, and my eyes widened. Someone had been in my house and placed a bug in my room.

What do we do? I mouthed.

He carried the device into my living room and took several pictures. Then he looked through my kitchen drawers.

Finding a meat tenderizer I didn't even know I owned, he pulverized the device. Then he bagged it up wrapped in a paper towel. I watched him carry it out to his motorcycle and toss it in the top-box, locking it in.

"I'm going to finish checking your room and then we'll talk," he said after he closed and locked the door.

I sat on the couch waiting for him to get back. Once he came back with nothing else in hand, I sighed a sigh of relief.

"What now?" I asked.

"I sent photos of that to Kinkaid and some of my other contacts. I'll also hand over the device to Kinkaid. He knows I destroyed it, just in case. Hopefully, I won't get in too much trouble." He winked at me. I didn't find it humorous.

"Logan," I warned.

"Right, winking, sorry. Anyway. Now, I think we look through all the journals from your mom. See if they have any information. We have to figure out who is doing all this. Now that they've escalated to murder, I have no doubt they won't hesitate with you once they have what they need."

Now that they've escalated to murder, I thought. *Great. Now, it was about more than money, and I'm the one they want.*

"So, you think whoever is behind all this was just using that guy? You don't think it's him?"

"Honestly, I don't know. It might be him, but we won't know until Kinkaid gets more information. But, I do think it's too convenient that he just happened to get murdered after everything. I think more likely a partnership. The good thing is the partner might lay low for a bit, regrouping."

"Okay, I'll go get the journals. I've already looked through one and it had nothing. We can each take one of the others."

I brought them to the living room, and we settled in, me on the couch, Logan on the floor with this head resting next to my legs.

"What was the name of the family with the money? The one that thinks their money went missing?" I broke the silence, my eyes glued to the story my great grandma had written on these pages.

"The family was Winter. Why? Find something already?"

"Actually, yeah, I think so. Read this. It's almost too crazy to be true. I would almost think she's writing a novel."

He took the journal and read. He read past what I did and then thrust it back at me. He pulled out his phone and typed a message to someone, probably one of his contacts, and then started doing some research on his own.

While he followed this lead, I kept reading. I couldn't believe the story she'd weaved. The life she'd lived. The events that had happened. My heart broke for her, and I was impressed by her finesse for self-preservation. A trait I could really use right about now.

I still couldn't put together how this led to our circumstances today, but it looked like Logan was right. This was all about money. Money I didn't know about. Money I had no access to. And, family. Family I never even knew existed.

Chapter 17

THE NEXT COUPLE OF days were pretty uneventful. I ran the bookstore, and Logan worked from my back office chasing down our new leads. He and Kinkaid got together a few times to go over some details. Bridgette made sure to bring me meals. Usually, she or Logan would sit and make sure I ate a little bit, too.

I had Persephone and Olivia work a few shifts with me, too, just to take a bit of a break. Breaks I usually spent sitting in the back office with Logan while he worked. I kept a close eye on Persephone, who seemed as jumpy as I felt. Something I worried had nothing to do with my own recent events.

Early Thursday afternoon, Trent came into the bookstore. I did a double take because I'm fairly certain I'd never seen him in the bookstore before.

"Hey Trent. Can I help you find something?" I asked.

"Oh, no, not much of a reader. Sorry," he looked absolutely apologetic, and I wasn't sure if I wanted to give him a hard time about it or spare him. I decided to spare him, since we'd never had that joking relationship.

"It's okay. Honest. What can I do for you?"

"This is more of a social call. I wanted to see if you and Logan are free tomorrow night. We're getting everyone together at the pub while Shiloh is in town. Also, because I have a surprise for Calliope, and I want all her friends there for it."

I swear I saw blush creep into his cheeks and up his ears. I knew immediately what he must have planned, and I was so happy for my friend. Anyone else might seem to be moving too fast, but these two were basically divinely inspired, so it made sense.

"We wouldn't miss it for anything. Honest."

"I know what she's going to say, but I'm still nervous. Is that weird?" He asked.

"No. Not at all. I think I'd be more worried if you weren't nervous. You two will be very happy together. Thanks for letting us all be a part of your night," I beamed.

"Oh, also, she's been really busy this week with wrapping up her teaching, and she wants all the details about where your case is. You will probably have to share your updates with everyone tomorrow. Just so you have a heads up."

"Won't that kind of talk ruin your evening?" I asked. The last thing I wanted was for my own nonsense to be a damper on a special night of my friends.

"Are you kidding? I think the distractions of two different kinds of excitement are what she needs to destress the week she's had at school."

"Whatever works," I said, stifling a little giggle.

After Trent left, Persephone came in for her shift, but her eyes were hollow. She wasn't even making eye contact, keeping her head down as much as possible.

"Hey, are you okay?" I asked. We hadn't talked much since everything happened. Mostly just about the guy who was in here. I was honestly ready to make someone else's problem my own to take my own off my mind.

"I don't know. I think I'm just tired. I keep misplacing things. Keep thinking I'm hearing or seeing things. I feel like I'm going crazy. Is that grief? Is that what grief does? I'm used to being so strong, self-reliant. Lately, I don't know. I keep wanting to be alone, but not. If that makes sense. It has to be grief, right?"

I thought back to losing my grandparents and my mom's mom. What was grief like for me? I don't think I was quite so scattered, but what did I know? I wasn't a professional. From my experience, grief affected people differently.

"Honestly? I don't know. Grief doesn't really have a typical appearance, I don't think. I think it just takes time."

She didn't look at me, just took her place behind the counter. Part of me wanted to just close up and give her time, but I also knew sometimes working helped distract from grief. My heart broke for my friend.

"I just wish I didn't feel so weak, so insecure. I've never felt this way before," she finally broke the silence.

"Time, I think. Just takes time." It was all I could think to say. I felt insecure all the time, so I couldn't help her there. I squeezed her hand before going back to check on Logan.

"Find anything?" I asked taking the seat across the desk from him.

"Actually, yes. I think it all makes sense now. We just don't know who we're looking for. It could have been that guy, I guess. Though it's still more likely he had a partner."

"Okay, so, what happened?"

"So, like her journal said, she left with some money. Became someone else. I think that money is hidden somewhere, the key passed down through your family. We just need to find it. As for the Winter family, they lost everything in the next couple of generations. Kind of fell off the face of things, but I'd guess someone from the most recent Winter generation is looking for the money that your great-grandmother took. They must think they deserve it. Or, that it's rightfully theirs and not hers."

"Do you think they knew she was given the money? Do you think they think she stole it?" I asked.

"I would guess it doesn't matter either way. Whoever it is, they know about it and think you have it. Since it's just you and your mom left, that's probably why they went after you."

"But, it's not just us. My aunt is still living. She just doesn't really have a relationship with us. Didn't have much of one with my grandma, either."

"Maybe that's why she's not a target. Or maybe they went after her first. What all did you say you all inherited when your great-grandma and grandma died?"

"The journals, some paintings. I have one, Aunt Susan has another. The rest of them went to some art programs and charities that my great- grandma was part of. I don't know, the rest was just like the usual. Clothes. Dining sets. Stuff we didn't keep."

"None of that sounds like it's worth millions," Logan said.

"It's not. And, there wasn't any weird banking info that I know of. No keys. No safes. Nothing like that. My great-grandparents lived modest, but comfortable lives. As did my grandma, and now my parents. I still don't get where the money went."

I dropped my head. The world was spinning, and all I wanted to do was get back to my house to read the journal again. Though, I didn't know what else I'd find. I'd already read it cover to cover four times. Even with this new information, unless we could trace the Winter family line, we had no more suspects than we did before this break in the case.

And, now that we knew the money did exist, I felt even more like a sitting duck, waiting for someone to come get me. For my money. For money that just wasn't with my family anymore.

Logan came around the desk and lifted my face to his eyes. "Kassidy, I've got friends tracking down the family to the most recent generations. We'll find someone, the link to all of this. I promise. Okay?"

"Okay," I said, relying on his confidence to build my own.

"Look, I've hit a wall here. Why don't you close down early, and let's go back to your house. You can reread the journal, which I'm sure you want to do. Then, we'll watch some kind of comedy to make you laugh. Then, tomorrow, we'll hopefully wake up to more answers."

That made sense. I went to let Persephone know she could head home. She seemed reluctant but didn't argue. She just gathered her stuff and left. I locked up and led Logan to the general store.

"What are we doing here?" He asked.

"I'm going to make dinner tonight. I make some pretty great chicken dishes. Do you like pasta?"

"Yes, pasta is fantastic."

I got all the things I needed for the dinner and took it to the counter. Gideon glanced between us. I hated when he was the one working. I'd rather face his ex-wife, who still worked here, or Olivia.

"Nasty business, murder, isn't it?" he asked as he rang me up.

"It sure is but, I'm sure Detective Kinkaid will figure it out. Logan's been giving him some help, too. So, the murder won't go unpunished."

"I'm so sure. Just be sure you children aren't getting into things you can't get out of."

"I don't know if you are aware, sir, but we're not children. None of us has been for years now," Logan corrected him.

"Indeed," Gideon said, giving Logan a side eye.

We finished the transaction in silence and went back to my place. Logan searched the house as I cooked. He'd done that both nights since we found the bug. Tonight, I just wasn't surprised anymore. I also wasn't surprised he didn't find anything.

"So, where is the painting your great- grandma left?" He asked, watching me cook.

"It's hanging in the hall between the doors." I gestured that direction.

He disappeared down the hall again. I got the chicken out of the pressure cooker and prepared the salads as the spaghetti finished up. I heard movement, and guessed he was taking the painting off the wall and putting it back.

He came back to the kitchen shaking his head. "Nothing out of the ordinary, there. Just a homemade painting. It's lovely, but nothing special."

"Grab some plates?" I asked as I drained the pasta. "It's special because she painted it."

He grabbed the plates and set them on the island. I started plating the food for us, and we took it to the couch.

"I mean, beyond that. It's not a painting worth anything is what I mean. Money wise."

"Yeah, I know. But, money isn't the only thing that makes something special. Just wanted to remind you of that."

"Got it," Logan said, taking a huge bite. "This is amazing. Why have we only been eating food from the pub this whole time?"

"I don't know. Just easier, I guess. I like to cook, and when you're not buying food for me all the time, I usually eat most meals at home."

"Well, from now on, I'll just save my money and stock your pantry in there." He shoved another mouthful in his mouth.

I laughed. "You're on, Hart."

Though I was used to my own cooking, something about having someone else enjoy it made it taste that much better to me. While we ate, we watched some comedy special on one of the streaming services, and I forgot all about reading the journal again. Having an evening of just spending time with Logan, not thinking about the case, was exactly what I needed.

We pushed the plates away to finish the show, and I cuddled up next to Logan. He put his arm around me, and I felt like home. We stayed there, as if this was what we always did on a Thursday night, until the show was over. When the credits rolled, Logan broke the contact and picked up our plates.

"Hey," I said as Logan cleaned up from dinner. "Trent wants us to go to Brew & Bake tomorrow night for dinner. Everyone will be there. It's a special night."

"Oh, yeah? He planning to pop the question?" Logan cocked an eyebrow.

"Actually, yes. I already said I'd be there. And, since we all know you won't let me go alone, I told him you'd be there, too."

"Wouldn't miss it," he said, finishing the dishes.

I settled back into my couch. As weird as it was, in that moment, I was content. As if there wasn't a bunch of family secrets I'd never known or a crazy person after me. I had Logan and my friends. Once all this passed, they would all still be there for me. And, hopefully, Logan would still be right here, cleaning up after I cooked for us. Because he wanted to be, not because he had to be. Because I wanted him to be right here with me from now on.

CHAPTER 18

BREW AND BAKE WAS lively the next night. The day had passed ordinarily enough. No news from Kinkaid or Logan's contacts. We just worked and got ready for a night out.

This was an open mic night, and Calliope had a set scheduled. Her's was first, so I wasn't sure what Trent's plan was, but we were all there for it. The excitement was palpable between all our friends. We took up our usual booth, but along with the Dark Autumn band members, we had to add on a table.

Persephone looked in higher spirits, and it was clear she and Sebastian were basically an item. Ben even seemed to have let it go. I noticed Calliope talking to another woman by stage, someone she clearly knew, and that woman had all of Ben's attention from afar at the moment. I smiled to myself.

"I'm going to go wish Calliope luck," I told Logan as he settled at the booth. He nodded and turned to talk to Griffin, who seemed to have something important to share.

"Callie, good luck tonight!" I squealed as I approached the stage.

"Kassidy, thanks. Let me introduce you to Tarryn. She and I have toured together a lot. She came out to surprise me this weekend. Can you believe it?"

"No, that's great. Nice to meet you, Tarryn." I held out my hand and cast a quick glance at Trent. The guilt was all over his face. He really had thought of everything tonight. Calliope deserved him.

"Nice to meet you, too. I wish I had gotten here earlier today. I want to see your bookshop. I love reading, and it sounds so cute!" She gushed. It felt strange to have someone so excited about my business.

"Well, we're open for a few hours on Saturdays, so have Callie bring you by tomorrow. I'll be there from nine to twelve."

"We'll be there," Tarryn said excitedly. I liked her already.

"I'll leave you two to it. Gonna be a great night. Nice break from it all."

Calliope gave me a knowing look and a hug. I went back to the table just as Bridgette announced Calliope's performance set. Calliope was amazing, as usual, but our whole table seemed to all be waiting for the same thing. We all knew it was coming, but our friend had no clue.

At the end of her set, Calliope moved to get down, but stopped as Trent approached the mic.

"Before we go back to the table, there's something I want to do." He turned to Calliope, who looked confused but also suspicious. "Calliope, I wanted to do this the morning after you found me in the community center. I want you in my life for good. You're one of the best things that's ever happened to me, and I want to spend my life trying to be one of the best things that happens in your life. Will you marry me?"

He dropped down to one knee and fished a small box from his pocket. When he opened it, the lights by the stage made it sparkle and glint around the whole room.

"Of course, I will," she gasped as he slipped the ring on her finger. He scooped her up for a kiss as the whole crowd erupted in cheers. I looked at Shiloh and realized we both had tears running down our cheeks.

Trent led her off stage to Tarryn and then to his aunt and uncle, who I hadn't even realized were there. Tarryn met us at the table, where we all waited to give our congratulations. They joined us and our table started talking all at once. No one else seemed to bat an eye at the noise, as Bridgette brought over everyone's food and then settled in on the other side of me.

After a lot of talking about engagements and dresses and best times of year for weddings, I was starting to hope that Trent was wrong. I hoped Calliope would be too distracted to ask anything about what had been going on with me. No such luck. Once the din had settled and we were all halfway through our meals, she turned to me.

"Okay, don't think I've forgotten what's been going on around here. Please tell me you know more. You have answers? I hate that this kind of danger is back in town."

I noticed at the mention of danger, something flashed in Persephone's eyes. No one else seemed to notice, as all eyes were on me, waiting for explanation.

"We could just keep talking about how exciting things are for you, now, in the best of ways," I said.

"No such luck, Kass. Let's hear it," Shiloh said. Griffin gave her a smile and nodded.

I looked at Logan and Bridgette, and then decided to share what we knew about my family.

"My great grandma's name was Darlene Winter when she was born. But something happened that caused her to have to leave her family. She changed her name to Lanna Winthrop, and then married James Blackwell. Her family was wealthy. Really wealthy. It was old money from oil or energy or something like that."

I looked around the table at all my friends and Tarryn, watching them carefully as I spoke. Sebastian kept super close to Persephone, as if protecting her from whatever I'd say. Trent and Calliope sat together, taking as little space as possible, but listening to every word. Griffin had taken Shiloh's hand. Everyone was listening to the story, all seeming almost as invested as I was.

I took a deep breath and continued. "She was dating someone once. Someone rich and powerful from her circle. He had a dark side and darker secrets. He was controlling. Evil. Just vile, and she had to get away fast. She had to protect herself."

My eyes landed on Persephone and it all suddenly clicked. What's been going on? A deep knowing flitted through her expression, and I swear Sebastian pulled her closer, as if that was even possible. Like he was shielding her from my words.

I kept going. "Anyway, her father found out everything that was going on and helped her escape. He gave her her part of the inheritance. At least, what it was at that point. He helped her get away, change her name, save herself. She cut ties after that, disappeared into the night. She became Lanna Winthrop. Then married my great grandpa. They lived happily ever after."

I stopped, not knowing where the story really went after that. Except that the next few Winter generations lost their money.

"So, there really was money?" Bridgette asked, incredulously. Her voice dripped with giddiness that caused me to giggle. It was a great release of tension.

"It seems there really was money. And she's why some of it really 'disappeared.' Though, the Winter family ended up losing the rest of their money. That wasn't on her, nor does it have anything to do with me."

"So, then, who's coming after it now?" Shiloh asked, eyes wide.

"It's got to be one of them," Griffin said. "One of the Winter kids. Logan, do you have that family tree?"

"It's a big family, it kind of splinters over the last few generations. We're narrowing it down, but nothing yet."

"The other question then becomes how did they find you?" Griffin asked.

We all went silent. It was a question I hadn't even wanted to consider. How did they find me? And, what did they know that I didn't, or think that I knew they didn't. Having the question uttered out loud was like a punch in the gut.

"I really wish I knew. It makes no sense. There were no ties, no communications after that. It was one thing she regretted on her death bed. She didn't even go see her dad when he died. He rescued her, and she didn't even get to say goodbye."

Tears slipped from my eyes, and I noticed Calliope's tears matched my own as she grasped Trent's hand. I felt so bad for ruining such a special night with my story.

"Callie, I'm sorry to ruin your night. None of you should have to worry about this. I'm sure it's going to be figured out soon."

"Nonsense," she said. "Between the engagement and this story, which is crazy, by the way, it's so much more exciting than having to close out my classroom so the sub can take over for the rest of the year. This story is going to help me get through my last week next week."

I looked around the table. Bridgette looked as if her blood was boiling. "Why isn't Kinkaid doing anything?" She spat out.

"He is," Logan said, defense thickening his voice.

I recognized this anger from Bridgette. It was a mix of things, and I knew her issue with Kinkaid had nothing really to do with how he was handling my case. Poor Bridgette, always too far in or just on the edge when it came to guys.

Persephone excused herself, and Sebastian let her go. It looked as if it might actually kill him to do so. Ben looked shell-shocked. I didn't think that was possible since his dad was a cop and his brother, Seth, was military, but here we were. And poor Tarryn looked as if she'd just fallen into the twilight zone.

"I swear, it's not usually this exciting around here, Tarryn," I said, trying to calm her. Ben's head snapped to her, and his easy smile fell right back into place.

"No, I love it. I mean, I don't love it for you, that sucks. I'm so sorry this is happening. But there might be a song here."

We all laughed. Funny how life can be so serious and scary one moment, but with the right people we can find a breath of fresh air in it all.

"Money can do a lot, you know. You'd be surprised what money is worth to some," a cold voice came from behind the next booth over. It sucked all joy from the air, and I felt Logan stiffen next to me.

Trent was out of the booth before anyone could process anything. "Listen, old man, if you have anything to do with this, too, there's not a place you'll be able to hide in this entire state."

A hint of the old Trent was coming out. The one he'd been spending the last few years trying to distance himself from. Yet, his desire to protect his woman and her friends was winning out to his self- control.

Olivia's attention was snapped back to reality at this exchange. She'd kind of faded out during the story, attention divided as she tried to watch out for Persephone. She rushed between Trent and her father. "Look, calm down. He's just eaves dropping and trying to get a rise out of us. That's all."

She pushed Trent back a bit, staring down her father, and Huxley next to him. His disturbing shadow.

"And, I see it worked," Gideon smirked at Trent, then directly at me. Logan's hand grasped mine protectively.

Trent's not known for backing down, but then again, neither was Gideon. And I couldn't shake the feeling that this vile man had his hand on every bad thing that had been going on the last several months.

Calliope went to her man's side, "We're going now. Kassidy, thank you for coming out to

celebrate with us. I'll see you tomorrow and I hope it all gets sorted soon. Tarryn, you coming?"

Tarryn nodded and got up as Calliope took Trent's hand and led him toward the door. Sebastian took this as his cue to go find Persephone, and since Tarryn was gone, Ben followed.

I was left with the rest of my friends. With the concerned looks on everyone's faces and Gideon's laugh reverberating around us, I turned into Logan's chest and sob.

I could just make out Gideons next words. "You children are always trying to play in games you can't ultimately win." He clucked his tongue at us.

"Get out of here," Olivia ground out, and he must have listened because I heard him shuffle away, with Huxley right behind. I could make out Olivia's steps as they headed in the direction of her other friends.

"You're right, you know," I finally heard Bridgette say. "No money is worth this. We'll figure it out."

Logan's phone buzzed and I finally looked up. I nodded at Griffin and Shiloh as they put down their money and slid out of the booth. Bridgette got up to go back to work, too, having used her break and then some to spend time with all of us.

It was almost as if Gideon's words were enough to remind us that someone was always watching. Always listening. I didn't blame anyone for wanting to get out of here.

"Hey," Griffin turned back to me. "Get me a copy of that journal, and I'll get to work on that family tree, too. Some of the newspaper's resources may help. I know Logan's guys are on it, but too many eyes can't hurt."

"Yeah, I'll get it tomorrow," I said. Turning to Logan, I asked, "who was it?"

"Kinkaid, he has something for me. He wants to meet me at my office tonight. Something about the scene of the murder. He has some information that might help us find who's doing this. Wants me to look into it since his office will take a bit longer than private resources."

"What if this never ends?" I asked.

"It will. I'll make sure of it," he promised. An uneasy feeling settled over me.

Something about this spot right next to him felt like the only safe place. I didn't want to leave. But I also had no desire to go to his office. I just wanted to be home, in my bed, with him keeping guard on my couch.

"I don't want to go to your office, Logan. I just want to go home."

"Well, it's been quiet the last few days," he said, considering my words. "I don't know. It might not be safe."

"Look, I'll go straight home. I'll go inside and lock the doors. I won't open for anyone but you. You just come straight back after you talk to Kinkaid. If anything goes wrong, I'll be sure to call you first."

He considered my words. We both knew he couldn't force me to do anything, and we really needed a break in the case. "Okay, straight home. Don't stop and don't let anyone in except me. I'll hurry with Kinkaid and be right over."

With that, he paid for us and walked me to my car. The uneasy feeling returned as I listened to his motorcycle race away; and suddenly, I regretted not having him with me. Anywhere away from him felt unsafe now.

CHAPTER 19

My breath hitched as I pulled into my driveway. The door was halfway open, and light pooled through. I dialed Logan as I got out of the car.

"Logan, someone's in my house," I whispered.

"Don't get out of your car, turn around," he demanded. Panic was clear in his voice. He was all the way on the other side of the island. He'd let me come alone. We both assumed I'd be safe.

"I'm already out of the car. I'll get back in and drive away," I whispered as I turned back to my car.

I'd almost made it when I felt the gun at my back. "I wouldn't do that if I were you."

I gasped and dropped my phone. I could hear Logan off somewhere, but my focus was on the feminine voice behind me. One I'd come to know very well.

"Let's go, we're going to have a little talk." She grabbed my arm and turned me, gun still pressed to me. She stomped on my phone as she led me away from my car and into my house. I could only pray Logan could get here in time, and with Kinkaid, too.

"What are you doing, Jessi?" I asked.

"Shut up, princess, let's move."

Jessi threw me into my vanity chair and tied my hands behind my back before tying my feet to the chair legs. She trained the gun on me and backed toward the front door, which she closed and locked.

"Who are you?" I asked.

"I'm Jessica Northrop. My great-great- grandfather was Elvis Winter, you know that name?" She studied me.

I didn't know the first name, but I had to assume it was Darlene's father. I shook my head, honestly.

"You're a little liar. I know you know him. You have the rest of my family's money and I'm here to claim it. It's not her's, never was. She manipulated them to get it. I deserve that money. No one in my family was supposed to grow up the way we did. We were meant to have that money. So, you're going to give it to me."

"Jessi, I don't have any money. Whatever you think you know is wrong. And, I don't have any money to speak of."

Jessi started pacing. Something told me she was missing information, just like I was. I hated that she'd been living right next to me, this whole time. And, she even had a key. That stupid key. She had her own way in and out.

"I know you guys have been looking for it. You knew about the Winter family. I heard you."

"Because you bugged my house!" I was livid. This woman had no right to anything she was claiming. Gideon was right, though, the lengths people will go through for money. "How did you even find me and my parents? How did you know about Darlene and who she became?"

"Kills you not knowing something, doesn't it?" She smirked and kept pacing. Finally, she stopped, and trained the gun back at me. "No more questions, Kassidy. Tell me what you know, now. I'm bored and I'd like to get out of here before anyone else comes. I know your bodyguard can't be too far behind. How naive of you to come home without him, anyway. Let your guard down after I got rid of that punk Drews, didn't you?"

"Jessi, I don't have money. Neither does my family. My great-grandmother got rid of it somewhere along the way. No idea how or where, but she didn't have much to leave us. And, that money was rightfully hers. Her father saved her and gave her what she needed to survive."

"Lies. That's all just lies he told because she was the favorite, meanwhile my great grandpa was a nothing to him. That money was his, rightfully, since she just left. Give me my money."

She started pacing again, gun glancing my way every so often. Panic was rising. Someone had given her a bitter story that didn't match with what we'd already learned. She was too caught up in being entitled to the money to realize she wasn't thinking straight. How do you argue with a madman?

I tried to undo the tie around my hands. She'd done some great knot work back there, and I couldn't loosen it. Duct tape would have been preferable, as I think I could have ripped it. This rope was too much, though.

"Stop moving, and tell me what you know," she demanded, turning the gun back on me.

"I have told you all I know. It's not my fault you're crazy and don't believe me. Whatever happened to the rest of your family's money, huh? Because that dried up real quick, didn't it? You can't be the only one of your generation that suffered, so why are you here banging down my door? How did you find me?"

"I guess I'll just have to rip your house apart again, won't I? Find those journals you were talking about. Get the answers from your lying Darlene herself. Now, where should I start?"

Jessi looked around the living room, and seemed as if she'd move toward the office when we heard a banging on the front door.

"Police, open up!" I heard Officer Hasting's voice shout. What was he doing here?

Jessi started to panic, waving the gun around. It finally landed on me. "Don't make a sound," she hissed.

I clamped my mouth shut, biting my tongue to prevent from screaming out. If I screamed, I was certain she'd shoot me before anyone had a chance to get to me.

"Open the door or we're coming in!" Hastings shouted again, banging on the door.

Jessie rushed behind me and aimed the gun at my head, arm around my neck. I didn't move, barely even dared to breathe.

"Come in and I shoot her. You don't want that, do you?" Jessi shouted.

The world stopped. I knew this was how it ended for me, and I hated it. I didn't want it to end without Logan here. It was all I could do to keep composed as the seconds passed but felt like hours.

"Drop the gun," I heard from the hallway. Kinkaid was in my living room. I don't know how he got in, but I didn't care. Jessi swung her gun toward him as the front door busted open. Jessi swung her gun to Hastings and tightened around my neck.

"Don't do something stupid, ma'am," Hastings said. He wasn't in uniform, but Kinkaid was. I had no idea why they were both here. But I was so thankful.

Jessi lowered her gun and released my neck. Suddenly, Logan was in front of me. He went behind and untied my arms and as soon as he was in front of me again, my arms were around his neck. He'd brought the cavalry, and it was finally over.

I heard Kinkaid reading Jessi her rights and alerting the station to the arrest. Apparently, he had been off duty and needed someone to come secure the suspect. He pulled gloves out of his pocket and bagged the weapon, as well as the ropes that had been around my arms. Logan moved aside so Kinkaid could untie my ankles with gloved hands.

"I'll need your prints to rule out from the ones on the wrists," he told Logan, who agreed.

Logan scooped me into his arms. "You're safe, sweets. I've got you."

Suddenly the space was filled with deafening sounds. The sirens. Jessi's demands. Officers moving in and out. But, all I could focus on were Logan's words. I was safe.

He was here. He and Officer Hastings and Detective Kinkaid had saved me. It was finally all over. I knew at some point I'd need to process that it had been Jessi this whole time, and I'd invited her to live right next door. Literally giving the devil a key.

But, right now, I wasn't ready for that. It was too much. I just wanted to focus on Logan's arms around me, his voice in my ear.

An officer came over to Logan and me. "Not now, Grant," Kinkaid said. "They'll come by first thing in the morning and give their statements, okay. Not now."

The officer glared at Kinkaid but backed off. I was so thankful. Giving a statement was the last thing I wanted to do that night. After everything. I just wanted to let it all be over.

"I can't stay here until the locks are changed," I told Logan.

"Do you want to go to Bridgette's? Or do you want me to stay on the couch again?" He asked.

"I think a night with Bridgette will be good. You go home. Come get me first thing in the morning. We'll take the 6 am ferry to the police station and then come back so

I can finally open the shop without all this hanging over me."

"Kinkaid, I'm taking her. Make sure to close up when you leave," Logan said. A nod of understanding passed between the two, and Logan took me out of the nightmare.

CHAPTER 20

THE NEXT DAY, BRIDGETTE made me coffee as she prepared to go help with the baking at Brew & Bake. "I can't believe it was her the whole time. Did she ever say how she knew about you?"

I took the mug and added sugar and cream. "No, she didn't answer any of my questions. Just kept yelling at me and calling me a liar. I have no idea how she found out. Maybe Kinkaid and his team have gotten that bit out of her by now. I'm just relieved it's over."

"You don't think anyone else from her family will come after it, do you?"

"Honestly? I have no idea. In order to look at their family history and think they are that entitled has to take a special kind of insane, right? Delusional. But, it also means someone must have known the whole story, known she was that way, and took advantage."

"Who do you think would do that?"

"I wish I knew. But, I think it's over, really. I don't think anyone else will come after me now that all of this has gone down this way. My boyfriend is too protective for that."

We both stopped the minute the word was out of my mouth. Bridgette's mouth hung open. "Boyfriend?" She screeched.

"I don't know, it just came out. But it seems that way, doesn't it?" I asked, knowing she knew more about this stuff than I did.

"I mean, we've all been thinking it, but no one knew if you were. This is big, Kass. You haven't had a boyfriend since early college. I don't think he wants anyone else to have that title, so I think it's a safe one to give to him." She beamed at me.

I smiled back. My tormentor had been arrested and I had a knight in shining armor, who I'd soon ask about using the "boyfriend" word. My heart swelled at the thought, and there was a knock at the door.

"Speak of the white knight himself," Bridgette smiled, and went to open her door. "Come on in, Sir Logan, the best knight in shining armor we know. Thanks for rescuing my damsel, here."

Logan laughed and greeted me with a hug. "One damsel that was definitely worth saving."

If we were alone, I'd probably have kissed him, and he looked like he felt the same.

"Ugh, you two, get a room. That look is enough to melt my whole house. Now, don't you have a ferry to catch?" Bridgette shooed us out of her house.

When we were settled on the ferry, we went out to watch the boat sail along toward the mainland. "So, I'm worth saving, huh?" I asked, nudging him with my elbow. I didn't look at him, worried what I'd see there now that I was alone.

"Look at me, sweets. I need your eyes when I tell you this," he repeated his words from the park the other day. I looked up, his blue eyes so intense. "I would save you over and over if it means a chance at a future with you. One without break ins and a stalker next door. I would save you as many times as it takes to be able to stand right here and tell you I'm not going anywhere. And, I'd like to kiss you."

I leaned up, letting him close the distance. His lips met mine, tentative at first but then deepening. I didn't want the kiss to end. I didn't want to reach the mainland and face the evil that was wanting there. I just wanted to stay wrapped in his arms, his kiss causing all kinds of warmth inside. It was the sweetest, most amazing kiss I'd ever had, and I didn't want it to end.

He pulled away too soon, but then engulfed me in his arms. "I'm not going anywhere, Kassidy. Now that I'm in your life, you're stuck with me. And, not to get ahead of myself, but I plan to do for you exactly what Tent did for Calliope one day. So, if you think catching Jessi means I go away, it doesn't."

"You think you're gonna marry me one day?" I asked, backing up to look in his eyes. There was nothing but sincerity and passion there.

"I know I will. You're mine. We'll take our time to get there, but you're never getting rid of me. Once a man knows he has the best thing in the world, he's not going to let her go."

I beamed up at him. So glad to be in this moment here with him. I faced the mainland again, and Logan boxed me in with an arm on each side, grasping the railing. His chest rested near my back and his chin rested on my head.

"You know who you should tell that to?" I asked after a bit of silence.

"Who?"

"You should tell that to Griffin. Can't get any better than Shiloh. So, where's her happily ever after? He's ruined her for men forever, and I'm not sure he cares any-more."

"Oh, he knows. He cares. He's just slow. He'll get there."

"I hope so, they both deserve to be as happy as we are."

The announcer let everyone know to prepare to dis-embark and we returned to the car. The anxiety built as we got closer to the police station. I hated the thought of even possibly being in the same building as Jessi after everything. Knowing she wasn't just there for breaking and entering, but also murder.

"Kassidy. Logan," Kinkaid greeted as we entered.

"Hey, just starting?" Logan asked him.

"Yeah, I wanted to get a crack at her myself, and wanted to be the one to take your statements. Didn't think you'd be in this early. Give me a minute and I'll take you back for your statement."

He busied himself with some paperwork and stopped to talk to another officer before taking us back. Once we'd both shared all we could from the night before, he had information for us.

"So, Logan, what I was going to tell you is on the victim, a guy by the last name Drews, we found DNA. Somehow got a rush on it, at least partially. It came back as a familial match to you, Kassidy. Female. Obviously. So, Jessi's definitely our girl."

"How does Drews fit into this?" I asked.

"She hired him to do the dirty work. Most of it, anyway. Right up until he got greedy. Demanded more money, went rogue when he talked to Persephone, and then we had his picture. Jessi didn't like that, so she took him out and went to work on her own."

"Did she happen to say how she found out about Darlene? About me?"

"Oh, yeah. She thinks that will help her case somehow, even though we have her for conspiracy to commit theft, breaking and entering, murder. She's never getting out. But, you'll never guess. She said it was Gideon. He was her grandparents' lawyer. Gideon also represented the Winter family for a time. That's how he found out about it all."

My jaw hung open. A chill ran down my spine. Gideon knew. He knew the whole time. And he led her right to me.

"But, how did he know about Darlene?" Logan asked.

"Now, that one I'm not so sure about. Neither is she. Apparently, her branch of the family fell on some hard times. Her dad was kind of a deadbeat. Gideon must have been watching them. He must have known something somehow and knew to be watching. Once he needed something, he knew who would be manipulated the easiest to make you a target."

"Just like he did with Calliope."

"What's this guy's deal? Can you get him for anything?" Logan asked.

"He didn't break any laws as far as I can tell. He shared client information with client family who had rights to said information. He didn't tell her to do what she did, not exactly anyway."

"Gideon is a sleaze, but he's smart," I said. "He's been around for a while. It's possible in doing work as an attorney, he figured out what happened to Darlene and filed it away. He's got an agenda, but no one can figure it out. He's got something big planned, and Griffin's been trying to break the guy for years."

I looked down at my hands. Maybe none of us were really safe, after all. Not with Gideon around to bring our worst nightmares right to our doorsteps. Persephone flashed in my head. I had to wonder if he'd led someone to her, someone who was taking advantage of her grief and making her feel crazy.

"I don't know, but I have other news. The sheriff's office isn't too keen on the uptick in violent crimes out on the island. They are creating an outpost out there. I'm going to be one of the officers out there. Still a detective, but

I'll have my office out there. Hastings applied for transfer as well, and I think since he's been on scene both times, they'll accept. That means, we need a building." Kinkaid looked at Logan.

"Well, Griffin, Seth, and I just closed on the old mill. There's plenty of room to retrofit a sheriff's outpost along with our offices and security compound. If the state wants to draw up the contract."

"I was hoping you'd say that. I kind of like this cloak and dagger, vigilante stuff. May retire early just to join you guys." Kinkaid and Logan laughed, and I was lost.

"What?" I asked.

"Seth Hastings and I are opening a private investigative and security firm. The office I'm in now is just temporary until we get the old mill in shape. I guess now, it'll also be the Miller's Pointe police station."

"I guess it's nice we'll finally have law enforcement on the island, even if it is only nine to five," I said, hating that this much crime had happened to necessitate the change.

"Oh, we'll be on call, too. We're not leaving the town without protection. We'll also have eyes on Gideon and his organization, too. Which sources tell us may be down to just him, that Huxley guy and a small handful of others."

I felt better knowing the town wouldn't be facing Gideon without protection. None of us knew what he was up to or what he was capable of, but with a police presence and private security firm on the island, it wouldn't be easy for him. I was especially grateful now that it seemed his power was less than we all realized.

"Did Jessi say anything else?"

"Just that her family didn't believe the story about the boyfriend. Seemed like a good guy. They just thought Elvis was spoiling his princess. Doesn't seem likely to me. If I had a daughter who I apparently loved more than anyone, the only way I'd let her disappear would be to save her. I have to believe Elvis was the same way."

We said our goodbyes and Logan and I went to see my parents. I just wanted to let them know everything was okay and share what we'd learned. My mom was shocked. So shocked, she called my aunt to tell her everything that had been going on.

"Have her check the back of the painting," my aunt said. My mom had put her on speaker.

"The back of the painting?" I asked.

"Yeah, a while back I was moving mine and the paper lining the back ripped. Found some bank information. Didn't think much of it. But I think it's about a safe deposit box. Maybe she was paranoid enough to split things up between the paintings. You find the key, and I have the papers, we can go claim what's ours. Split it down the middle and be done with all of this. I'll even give you my painting."

My jaw dropped, mirroring my mothers. We hung up the phone, and my parents followed Logan and me to the ferry.

When we got to the house, we found Joe had already replaced the door that was kicked in and was changing the locks on both units.

"Thanks, man," my dad said, clapping his back.

I rushed to the painting and took it off the wall. Nothing out of the ordinary. The paper seemed to fit flush to the back. I shook it, no sound coming beyond the paper crinkling. I carefully cut the paper away and peeked in. There, taped to one of the cross boards of the canvas was a small key. I carefully took it out and lifted it up to show everyone.

"That's it. How do you think the safe deposit box is being paid for?" my mom asked. "Must be with the money she left there.

We'll have Susan call the bank and get us set up with an appointment. Maybe we can even get in today, if we're lucky."

My mom called my aunt who gave us the name of the bank. We waited while she called them, and called us back. We were able to get in that day, so we all rushed back to the mainland and down to Seattle where the bank was. I was so relieved they had long Saturday hours.

On our way, I arranged for Olivia to open the store, so I could keep my word to Tarryn that she could shop there. Given all that was going on, I was proud of myself for remembering.

Once at the bank, the manager met with us. "I need ID to open the box. I have four names on the box list. Lanna Winthrop, Rose Smith, Mary Smith, and Susan Smith."

"I'm Mary Smith, now Mary Winters. This is my sister Susan Smith."

"Don't suppose you have a marriage license or birth certificate with you to prove your maiden name?" he asked, looking like he wanted to let us in, but couldn't.

"Unfortunately, no, we just learned of this today."

"I have my ID. I'm still Susan Smith. And, she is Mary Smith. If I show ID, and they have the key, can we all go?"

"You two, and the young lady can go. The gentlemen will have to wait up here."

Logan stiffened. I knew he didn't want to let me out of his sight at the moment. My dad stepped in. "They'll be fine. We'll stay right here while you take care of this."

"Okay, let me see your ID, and I'll take you down. I'm aloud to release the contents to your care. What you do with it beyond that is between you and any lawyers that may be involved. Please, don't make me regret this."

My mom and Aunt Susan both gave agreement, and I followed quietly. We were led into a vault room, and the manager took out a small key that looked like ours.

"Okay, box 753. We use your key and the master key to open the box and free it from the vault. Who has the key?"

"I do," I said, handing it over. I held my breath as he opened the locks and retrieved the box. Finally, I'd get to see what all the fuss is about. Why the last few weeks of my life had been torture. It was all right here in this box. It was right there on my wall.

The manager placed the box on the table and used the key to open it. "Now, we've been taking monthly payments for the rental from the amount for the past forty-seven years. So, minus that amount, you have about four million dollars left here. Assuming you're taking it all today."

Our mouths all fell open. No one spoke for a long time. My mom finally broke the silence. "Four? Four million? As in, million?"

"Uh, yes, ma'am, that's how that works. Four million dollars."

"We get to take four million dollars home today? That's two million for each of us," my aunt said, awe in her voice.

"I guess, if that's how it's meant to be divided up, then yeah. You do. We don't own it. You do. Your name is on the box, it's yours."

My mom and my aunt exchanged glances. "You are going to split it, right?" My mom asked.

"Of course I am. We don't get along well, but I'm not a monster. Obviously, Kassidy deserves some of that money. If it weren't for everything that's been going on, we wouldn't even be here."

The manager looked uncomfortable and confused. But, once he talked to both my mom and aunt, he decided the easiest thing to do would be to just split the money evenly between them and wire it to their respective banks. I guess he decided he didn't need my mom's marriage license after all.

While they took care of the details, I filled in my dad and Logan on what we'd found. Their faces looked just like ours had when we heard, and I almost worried my dad was going to have a heart attack.

"All taken care of. Let's go home," mom said when they were finished.

"Kassidy, good to see you. I'm sorry for what you went through. Our family may not be the best communicators or anything, but you never should have gone through that. I hope something good comes out of this for you," Aunt

Susan said, giving me and mom a quick hug before she hurried out.

My parents took Logan and me to a late lunch, where they told me they'd be giving me half the money my mom had just gotten. A million dollars to go toward my bookstore, and any expansions I may want. I tried to argue, but they wouldn't let me out of it. I couldn't wait to tell the girls I'd be able to pay them off, especially since I'd been behind again thanks to Jessi's reign of terror.

As we said goodbye to my parents and headed back to Miller's Pointe, I marveled at how my world had changed. All because of some greedy distant cousin who led me to a wealth my family didn't even know we had. As we rode the ferry home, I leaned my head against Logan, so thankful he'd been by my side through it all.

CHAPTER 21

SUNDAY MORNING, WE ALL attended church at the pub. Odd, we knew, but since the community center burned down, that's where we were meeting. Trent and Calliope had taken over where her grandparents had left off as ministers; and I knew they had plans for Sunday service at the community center once it was rebuilt.

After service, Bud and Mabel always had a special meal for everyone. It was always like one big family, especially since we always claimed our favorite booth. One that was starting to get a little crowded with everyone.

Tarryn was still in town visiting and wouldn't be going home until that evening. Ben had been very attentive to her while she was here, but she seemed to eat it up. I didn't know much about her, but she seemed like she'd fit right in to this town.

Dark Autumn took the booth right to the side of our corner booth; right by one of the big picture windows. A booth I guessed would become their both as they spent less time in the game room, making way for the next generation. Tarryn sat right at the outside of our booth, just next to where Ben sat at the outside of their booth. Olivia next to him and Sebastian and Persephone across from them.

This morning, Persephone looked better than she had in days. The light was back in her eyes, at least a little bit. It seemed having Jessi caught gave us all a little relief.

I turned my focus back to the group around me. "So, what happens with the duplex now?" Calliope asked.

"I call it," Persephone hollered from her table.

"You want it?" I asked.

"I think so. Shiloh has to move back to the farmhouse, and now that Trent is around so much, I think it'll get crowded quick. I'm good for the rent and I'll try not to be loud."

I looked to Calliope. "Don't look at me," she said. "Perse is an adult. If she wants to move out, I can't stop her. Even if I think it's a bad idea given all that's been going on. She does make her own money, so."

"Well, Jessi's behind bars now, so," Bridgette said.

Calliope and Shiloh shared a look, one I couldn't read. But, it didn't look good.

"That's not what I was talking about." Calliope shot Persephone a pointed look. Persephone didn't falter. Confidence and hope were written all over her face.

"If you fill out the application so my parents can do the background check, you're in. I'd rather have you as a neighbor than a stranger any day. Plus, my dad can put a security system in for you, too, if you want."

"Sweet," Persephone pumped her fist. She and her friends started talking about her new place and how she'd be setting it up. Definitely a much better choice than my conniving distant cousin.

"Now that that's solved, another bit of news," I said, looking at Logan. He smiled widely, encouraging me to continue. "I'm about to come into quite a bit of money and I'll be able to pay the rest of the lease in full."

I looked at Shiloh and Calliope. They both got big smiles on their faces. I knew they were just as ready to have the lease up as I was, but they deserved to get paid what we'd agreed on after their grandparents passed.

"So, there really was money," Bridgette said.

"Crazy as the story sounds, there was. Jessi really was a distant cousin. DNA confirmed it. And, Lanna really did put the money away for her future family. She added my mom and aunt to the safety deposit box shortly before she died. Four million was left to split between the two of them. Now, I get a million of that. I should have it in a week or so. Once I pay off the building, I'll have just enough to expand my collections and broaden what I carry in store. I get to really make it something."

"Kassidy, I'm so happy for you. That's amazing. I'm sorry it took this whole ordeal to get here though," Shiloh said.

"Yeah, did they ever find out how she knew who you were, though?" Griffin asked.

"Unfortunately, yeah. It was…" I started before Olivia cut me off.

"It was him, wasn't it? My dad?" she asked, leaning over the top of her booth.

"Yeah. It was your dad. You got any idea why he's sending our worst nightmares our way?" I asked.

"I wish I did. I've been trying to figure it out. But, I've got nothing so far. Unfortunately, to find out, I think that means I have to go into the lion's den. I haven't been around him much since mom left four years ago. I'm not sure I can fake it enough to get the answers we all need."

"Don't get yourself in any trouble now. You might be his daughter, but I'm not convinced he wouldn't see you as any more than a pawn in his game. As much as I hate to say that," Griffin said.

"I know," Olivia said, tears in her eyes. She turned back to her table and both our tables fell silent.

"Man, I hate that guy," Trent said. We all murmured our agreement.

"Okay, well, I gotta get to work. The dining room opens to patrons soon, so I'll see you guys later," Bridgette said, shooing Trent and Calliope out of the booth so she could get out. "Kass, I'm so glad this is all over. And, I'm so glad some good things have come out of it." She nodded at Logan so I wouldn't miss her meaning.

He kissed the top of my head and I smiled. After a few minutes, everyone else filtered out slowly, too, ready to go about their Sunday. This left me alone with Logan, something I wasn't mad about.

"So, you think some good things have come out of this?" he asked, eyes intensely searching mine.

"Oh, I'd say that's a fair assessment. I get to buy my shop. I get to expand what I sell. I get to expand my collections. I don't have a psycho neighbor anymore. All good things." I stopped there, just to see what he'd say.

He feigned a look of offense. "That's it? That's all the good things? Nothing else good came out of this?"

He didn't let me answer before he planted a deep, long-ing kiss on my lips. I met his kiss with equal passion, and we stayed that way until we heard someone clear their throat.

"Get a room, you two," Bridgette laughed, picking up most of the plates from our table.

As she walked away, I looked up at Logan, "okay, there's also this guy. He's pretty amazing. He's my hero. I think I'll keep him around."

He gave me another quick kiss and said, "good. Because, I'm not going anywhere. Now, how bout we go find a place to enjoy this sunny, but cold day?"

"I can think of a few places," I said, taking his hand as we slid out of the booth.

We spent the early afternoon at the tide pools before heading home to watch something, allowing ourselves to let out all the stress we'd been carrying since this all started. As we were partway through our second movie, there was a knock on my door.

"What's this?" I asked, letting Bridgette into the house.

"This is your new guard dog, Mutt." Bridgette led the medium sized dog in behind her, holding the leash tightly. Mutt barked and sniffed at me before settling onto the floor near Logan's feet.

"I don't have a guard dog," I said. I glanced at the dog, who was definitely not a puppy, but seemed already to be perfectly at home, especially near Logan.

"You do now. I just adopted him for you. You need a guard dog."

"I have a security system. And, I'm not even allowed to have pets here, Bridge. Why did you bring me a dog I can't keep?"

Bridgette unhooked Mutt's leash. "You are now. I just talked to your dad, and he's in agreement. You need protection."

I looked incredulously at her friend. "So let me get this straight, you adopted a dog for me, then got my dad to agree to bend the no pets rule for me. All without talking to me?"

"That's the size of it, yeah," Bridgette smiled.

Logan chuckled from the couch while petting Mutt behind the ears. He was thoroughly amused, and Mutt clearly had no desire to be anywhere else.

"You gonna take care of him for me, too?" I asked, walking over to give his head a pat.

"No, you're on your own for that. You know I'm a cat person. But after the few weeks you've had, it's clear to me you need protection. Especially since Logan will have to go home, now. And, you just possibly need an emotional support animal. A dog can be both. Besides, I know you, Kass. You decided he could stay before you even knew he was yours, don't deny it."

I laughed at how much Bridgette really knew me. "You're right. But, did you at least bring me any supplies?"

"No, but Griffin and Shiloh will be here soon with some. He went to the pet store while I went to the shelter."

"Should have known you were in on it with someone else. Well, he seems perfectly content here, want something to drink?"

"I'll get it, you get to know your new roommate." Bridgette made herself at home in the kitchen, getting the three of us some water from the fridge. She gathered our favorite pretzels and hummus, knowing I always had them on hand.

Setting the food on the coffee table, she sat down and looked around. Shuddering, she said, "I can't believe you were a hostage here just a couple of days ago. How are you managing to stay here? How are you holding up, Kass?"

"Real talk? It's hard right now. I'm actually really thankful for this gift. I know I'm surrounded by neighbors, and neighbors I know well; but no one was here. Jessi was the closest neighbor. No one else heard or saw anything that could help me. Once she closed that door, that was it. I could have been a goner."

"Thank God for Logan." Bridgette took a sip of her water, reaching over to pat him on the arm.

"Yeah, thank God." I blushed at his name, smiling at him. I leaned my head on his shoulder, and he wrapped his arm around me. "I know it will all go back to normal soon, but I'm actually glad to have a dog to take with me around town. Who knows if there are any other looney's out there looking for the supposed riches."

"Yeah, so crazy how that all went down, but now you get to expand. What else would you do with any left over money?" Bridgette crunched on a pretzel, startling Mutt from his dozing.

"I'd help you start saving for the pub," I shrugged, not even having to think about it.

"You'd do that? With your money?" Bridgette asked, her eyes widened.

"Yeah, hasn't that always been the dream? I've already got The Bookshop. Now, we just have to make sure you're able to take over the pub so we can run this town."

Bridgette nodded, and we both let the thought go. It was a nice dream, but that's all it was. For now, we could just be content that order had been restored to our tiny town. And, now, another member had joined our ranks. I glanced at Logan again, as he pet the dog's head. Our little group was officially like the Scooby Gang, right down to the Mutt.

Dear Reader:

I HOPE YOU ENJOYED this return to Miller's Pointe as much as I did. Kassidy's story has been with me longer than the rest, and I loved bringing it to life.

As I've shared before, this little Pacific Northwest Island town is part of my heart, now. Its residents are so dear to me, and I hope you come to love them as much as I do. It is still my hope that as you continue the series, next with Persephone's story, that you'd see examples of hope in a dark world, and the beauty of community and friendship in the midst of life's mysteries and tragedies.

I have no plans to abandon this lovely town any time soon, and I hope to find you back here in each of my next books.

One note: reviews are so important to an author, so if you've got thoughts about this book, please leave one with your favorite retailer or the almighty Goodreads. This is such a huge thing for a small author, such as myself.

Also, if you want to follow along, see what happens to the gang next, and share a love of reading, writing, and

all things Pacific Northwest, join me over on Instagram or sign up for my newsletter (get yourself some bonus Miller's Pointe
goodies there). And follow along with Persephone's story in the next book, Frozen Hearts.

~ Candice Jeneé

ACKNOWLEDGEMENTS

To my author friends, thank you for never making me walk this path alone. I am so thankful to be making friends in the author community.

To Brooke from BY THE BROOKE DESIGNS, thank you for making such stunning covers for my words to live in. I could never make anything near as beautiful as you have.

To Sarra Cannon, thank you for blazing the trail and launching Publish and Thrive. The course has helped me have confidence in myself, my writing, and my author business.

To my mom and my husband, for being my first line of writing buddies and ventilators. I love you both.

ABOUT THE AUTHOR

Candice Jeneé is a lover of romantic suspense, feel good romance, and cozy romantic mystery. She is a former LMFT turned mental wellness coach running the Creative Mommas' Haven membership for creator moms. She writes clean/faith inspired romance and romantic mystery/suspense, along with some nonfiction.

Candice is a believer in rhythm over balance and strives for fulfillment and creativity in life. She lives in WA with her husband, two littles, and their cat, Pumpkin Pie. (Ironically, Candice isn't a fan of pumpkin pie the food.) She is a lover of elephants, waterways, and rainy days.

Other books by Candice

Miller's Pointe Romantic Mysteries & Suspense

Dark on Fire, Book 1
Deceit in the Sound, Book 2
Frozen Hearts, Book 3
Wrecked Hearts, Book 4
Careful Hearts, Book 5
Burning Hearts, Book 6

West Coast Crush Novellas

Savannah's Cowboy Crush
Harlow's Fake Fiancé
Serenity Snowed Inn (December 2023)